There are many tales today about dystopian societies. It's become a popular theme. These stories comprise books, movies and series. Few tell how the world changed from what is outside your door into such an unpleasant place, where you don't want to be. The Dead Series probes the depth of depravity, having already begun with Dead & Dead For Real. Dead Reckoning takes us down the path away from civilization. It's terrifying, because it takes little imagination to see the savagery coming. My research into bio-war and cyber war horrified me. We have little defense against them. Read on – get scared.

R. L. Clayton

"Far Out? Hell no! Dead Reckoning is a chilling story about what could happen to us today. Must Read!"
Larry Castriotta, author of We All Leak Eventually.

"R.L. Clayton's Dead Reckoning clearly illustrates the horror of an unconventional world war. You will be sitting on the edge of your seat as you read this thriller. Not to be missed!"
Alexis Powers, author of Kiss My Tattoo and Gotcha!!

"As the world slides into dystopia in this thrilling sequel to Dead, and Dead for Real, R.L. Clayton serves up more alarming science fact that shows who will survive, and it's not who you'd expect. Read it and prepare!"
Melinda Rucker Haynes, award-winning author of The Haunting of Josh Weston.

"From the window of Clayton's book, Dead Reckoning, I watched the world slide away from civilization and into chaos. He paints an all too real scenario. If it doesn't scare you, you're already dead."
Dr. Ted Dreisinger, PhD, author of Life in Small Bites and Life around the Edges.

"Kiki and Nick bring it, again. This time on a national scale--not to be missed." DeeAnna Galbraith, Author and Editor

By R. L. Clayton

The Evolution River Series
Sea Species
The Envoy
Genesis

Wings of the WASP

The Dead Series
Dead & Dead For Real
Dead Reckoning

Visit R. L. Clayton's websites
www.rlclaytonbooks.com
www.evolutionriver.com

For Linda, my wife. She's never read any of my books. What's with that? You hold things together while I'm lost in the worlds I'm creating. Thank you for being there.

I had not expected to write a sequel to Dead & Dead For Real, but as I completed it, I realized the characters weren't done telling me their story. Dead Reckoning is not the end of the "Dead" series. At least one more is under construction, and ideas are in bloom for more. The Tall Grass Editing Co Op is invaluable in converting my scribbling into a readable story. The members are all fine authors who inspire me. Our weekly meetings have become a treat.

My graphic artist, Steve Linebaugh, continues to produce great book covers, posters, newsletters, and artwork. Are we having fun, Steve?

Thanks to Bill Assenmacher and Caid Industries for lending support to my writing career.

Thank you all.

This book is a work of fiction. The characters, places, and incidents are a product of the author's imagination. Any similarity to actual people, organizations, or events is purely coincidental.

ISBN 9781948015127

DEAD RECKONING

Descent into Dystopia

Prologue

August 20

The Boeing 777 from Tokyo to Los Angeles had reached cruising altitude and the attendants were taking dinner orders. Anatoly Tsaryov watched his fellow passengers through slitted eyes, pretending to be asleep. The family in the five-by row across from him was trying to settle down, get the three kids in their seats.

"Mommy, I have to go to the bathroom," said the six-year-old girl. Her mom stood to let her pass into the aisle. The girl skipped down the aisle to the bathroom, her curls and pink dress bouncing in time.

Perfect, thought Anatoly. He withdrew a small pink bottle of My Bubbles from his carryon. As the girl returned, he pulled out the wand and blew a stream of bubbles into the aisle.

Her eyes got wide. "You want to blow some bubbles?"

She reached for the bottle, fingers flexing, then looked at her mom, her mouth open. He held out the bottle. Her mom nodded. Gingerly, she took it from him and blew a stream of bubbles into the air. They spread over the passengers near them, who began to laugh. The girl ran down the aisle, streams of bubbles in a cloud behind her.

Bubbles, yes. But much more, thought Anatoly. The solution contained the variola major virus, smallpox, the virulent form. By the end of the flight, most of the passengers would be exposed. Anatoly wasn't the only international jet passenger carrying My Bubbles bottles that day.

In the crowded immigration line, he gave a bottle to another child, a boy of five or six, who happily spread the bubbles over the laughing crowd, welcoming the diversion from customs. Airports in New York, Seattle, Atlanta, Dallas, Chicago and Washington, D.C. were all supposed to enjoy a bubble snowstorm.

The taxi dropped him off at his hotel. Crowds thronged the lobby, children's laughter drowning out the elevator music. While standing in line to check in, he watched an elevated monorail approach. He'd always wanted to see Disneyland as a child, and now he was being paid to visit it.

The receptionist smiled. "How may I help you?"

"I have a reservation under the name of Tsaryov. T-S-A-R-Y-O-V."

"Ah, yes. Here you are. Welcome to the Disneyland Hotel, Mr. Tsaryov." She smiled and glanced at her monitor. "I see we have a package for you. I'll have it delivered to your room."

His room was decorated with Disney characters. The view looked out toward the Magic Kingdom. The knock on his door interrupted his thoughts. It was his package. He tipped the bellboy and set the box on the desk. The packing slip listed Samples, My Bubbles.

Humming to himself, he put six bottles in his pockets and headed for the monorail terminal. Time to go to work.

Chapter One

September 9
Nogales, Arizona

Nicholas Sabino and Katherine Russell waited in the foot traffic line crossing the Mexican border in Nogales, Sonora. Nick, at six feet tall and slim, towered over Kiki's slender five foot-four frame. Both had dark hair and skin brown from being outdoors. Clutched in their hands were their counterfeit passports. Nick and Kiki had not been back to the United States in two years. Perhaps their fake deaths had fooled the authorities, but they had to assume they were still on the FBI's wanted list.

Had it not been for the critical illness of Nick's father, they would still be aboard their sixty-five foot trimaran, hopping islands in the southern Caribbean. The message from his brother came in on a shortwave broadcast five days ago. His father was gravely ill – not expected to recover.

Nick looked at the long line of returning American touristas and Mexicans going to the U. S. to shop. The immigration checkpoint was a danger. It made him anxious.

Kiki shared Nick's nervousness. "Think we'll be okay going through?" she asked. "I'm having mixed feelings about this return. Memories are surfacing I thought I'd buried."

"I'm feeling the same," agreed Nick. "Thank goodness Julio Cardenas came through with his promise. I had my doubts about trusting the head of a drug cartel, even if we did save his life."

Kiki nodded. "I didn't expect him to pick us up in his personal plane and fly us to Hermosillo. It saved us a lot of travel time."

Nick chuckled. "The luxury limo to Nogales was a little much. I was afraid it would attract the wrong kind of attention. It turned out okay. Julio is smart. After that private lunch at the restaurant, he had a taxi bring us to the La Roca bar, a block away from the port of entry."

"You do have the keys he gave you for the car?"

Nick nodded as they passed through the turnstile and handed their passports to the INS agent. The examination was perfunctory. Suddenly, they were on U. S. soil. Nick felt an urge to kneel and kiss the noonday sunbaked sidewalk.

In the parking lot a block away, they easily found the silver Lincoln Navigator. Minutes later, they were speeding along I-19 toward Tucson.

Kiki watched downtown flow past after merging onto I-10 toward Phoenix. The memories flooded in. So much had happened along this corridor to change and shape their lives. Kiki turned from the window toward Nick. His lips were pressed tightly together. "Gotta put this all to rest. Can't let it cloud the present or the future."

"Yeah, You're right. Wait til Mom meets you. You're going to like her. You're really going to like Da…" He stopped.

Kiki put a caring hand on his shoulder. They drove in silence.

As the car passed Marana, Kiki looked to the west. Her own ghosts rose. The memories of her family and the ranch were only a few miles away. The desert, interspersed with green farm acreage, passed by. It was unchanged. How could that be? Their lives were vastly different from the last time they had seen this land.

Certainly, they weren't the same.

Memories of her childhood on the ranch, her mom and dad, her husband and daughter flickered like an old black and white movie. She held onto the images, keeping the horror of their murders at bay. She closed her eyes. Her vision of the Arizona landscape faded, replaced by the desert of Afghanistan.

The soothing hum of the tires on the road became the roar of attack helicopters overhead, loosing rocket trails with explosions at the end. Fire and smoke reached for the sky from the town of mud huts and dirt streets five hundred meters away. The crackle of small arms fire set the melody to the staccato base of the machineguns hammering in the distance.

Through her twelve-power scope, Kiki watched robed men carry a heavy machinegun to a walled niche, hurriedly setting it up to ambush her advancing squad. Though she could not see the gunners because of the wall, she fired the Barrett Fifty with the explosive-tipped round. It blew a hole through the wall. The red smear on the wall behind told her she'd scored a hit, a normal action for Katherine Russell, top sniper in Afghanistan. With no further thought of that target, she sought others.

On either side of her, Corporals Dyson and Ling called targets and ranges as the enemy troops set up to repel her unit. Rather than offering cover, the mud and concrete block walls turned into deadly shrapnel as the fifty-caliber bullets punched through them. With the enemy huddled on the floor, her forces entered the town and fanned out, seeking the soldiers in a house-to-house search. When a bearded face peeked out, she fired. Whether she made a hit or not, the position was marked, the enemy unable to fire.

With the sound of the turn signal and the slowing of the car, she opened her eyes to Arizona again. Were they in Casa Grande already?

Chapter Two

September 9
Casa Grande, Arizona

Nick guided the SUV through the gate and up the steep twisting driveway. Behind and below, traffic moved on I-8 west. Suddenly, they were on a level parking area. He pulled into a shaded carport, seemingly part of the mountain. A wide eave shaded the doors and windows in the rock wall front of the large ranch style house. It was built into the side of the hill.

As they got out, stretching away the stiffness of hours in the car, Kiki looked north toward the city of Casa Grande. It was a magnificent view. She could see at least sixty miles. She turned at the sound of the front door opening. The slender silver-haired woman paused, looking at her then moved to Nick, clasping him to her. She seemed to wilt.

"It's okay, Mom. I'm here now." Nick held her. After several minutes, he turned her toward Kiki. "Mom, this is Kiki Russell, my," he paused, "my wife. Kiki, this is my mom, Miriam."

Kiki held out her hand, meeting the gaze of Miriam's teary blue eyes. "I'm so sorry to hear about Doctor Sabino's stroke."

"Nick, you never told us you'd gotten married." She clasped Kiki's hand and looked at Nick. "In fact, we never heard anything from you." Kiki detected reproach in her voice.

"I know, Mom. I'm sorry, but when I explain, you'll understand why we couldn't let anyone know where we were. But we're here now."

Miriam pulled Kiki's hand. "Let's go inside and out of this heat." She called over her shoulder, "Nick, you get the bags. Let's get some tea."

Kiki looked at Nick and smiled. It was the facial equivalent of a shrug. What else was she to do?

The tiled entryway opened into a large room with Southwestern flair. The furniture was heavy rough-cut oak with native-patterned cushions and pads. Indian rugs were on the floor, blankets hung on the walls. Shelves of baskets and pottery adorned the room. The back wall was a glass window with a view of the desert below and blue mountains in the distance.

Kiki was puzzled. The back wall should be against the mountain.

"It's done with mirrors," explained Nick, entering the room. "When Dad built the house into the mountain, he put a giant periscope at the back of each room to bring in light and a view. The top mirror is above us on the side of the mountain. The reflection from it hits the mirror you see there. If you look out the real window," Nick pointed toward the glass wall to one side, "the view is to the east. The mirrored view continues toward the south."

"Let's have our tea in the den," said Miriam. She turned away from Kiki. Her steps were sure as she led them down a stairway to a large kitchen. The countertops were granite with tiled walls behind. From a large pitcher of iced tea, Miriam poured three glasses. Nick led Kiki into the den. It too was Southwestern motif.

Seated before the glass doors, they looked across a swimming pool to a low walled patio. At one end of the pool, water cascaded from a rock structure. The wide patio eave extended nearly to the pool.

"This is a magnificent house," said Kiki. Her own humble ranch house came to mind.

"Rest for a few minutes, and I'll take you on the tour," said Miriam. They were silent, looking at the vista that seemed to stretch forever. Dust devils, slender tan towers, danced and wove their way across the valley floor. Though it was September, the beginning of fall in much of the country, in Arizona it was late summer, marginally cooler and much drier than August.

Nick broke the silence. "It's nice and cool. Your air conditioning system is working well."

"We just switched from the A/C to the cool towers last week when the humidity dropped. You know your father, he always had to be so green, keep the minimum carbon footprint." She turned toward Kiki. "Michael designed and built the house with the help of Nick and Stephen."

"Mom, we did have contractors," laughed Nick.

Miriam waved her hand in a dismissive gesture. "I know, but still, you all did a lot of the work." She turned back to Kiki. "The house is almost self-sufficient. We have solar panels and a wind generator supplying most of the power, with our own well for water."

"What's a cool tower?" asked Kiki.

"You probably didn't notice the towers at the ends of the house when we drove up," said Nick. "The cool towers are big pipes, thirty feet tall with spray nozzles at the top. By spraying water into the towers, evaporation cools the air and it sinks to the bottom. Ducts carry it throughout the house. The water comes from the storage tank on the hill above us. All the windows are triple pane glass, and the walls and roof are heavily insulated. That and being built into the mountain, there's very little heat load."

Kiki was a little overwhelmed by the explanation. It sounded complicated, but she could feel the cool breeze without the sound of a fan.

"It'll make more sense when I show you around," said Nick.

"Well, it sure works. What do you do in the winter?"

"It doesn't get very cold, but Michael put solar water heaters on the roof. We cover the pool with an insulating blanket and store the heated water in it. It's circulated under the floors throughout the house. Along with warm clothes and the heat-a-lator fireplaces, we don't get cold."

"Dad is really proud of this house." Nick glanced around the room and turned toward Miriam. "Mom, how is he?"

"I just got back from the hospital an hour ago. Stephen is with him now." Her eyes began to tear. "We need to go see him as soon as you are settled. He hasn't been conscious the last few days."

Nick looked at Kiki. "We'll be ready in an hour. Let me show you our room." He took her hand and led her down another flight of stairs.

The bedroom was a smaller version of the den, with a view to the west, the periscope mirror at the back giving a view to the north, bringing daylight into the room.

"Your wife?" asked Kiki when they were alone in the bedroom.

"I didn't know what else to say. Mom is old-fashioned that way. It was the easiest thing to say."

Kiki smiled. "Yeah, my parents were that way, too. Okay, we better get our story straight. Married in Aruba two years ago, bumming around since." She liked the sound of that. It was almost true, except for the ceremony and ring part.

"You know we'll have to give Mom and Stephen an explanation of what happened," said Nick.

"I know. Will the truth cause them trouble?"

"Our being here could cause them trouble. We owe them the truth."

Chapter Three

September 9
Casa Grande, Arizona

Nick's family gathered around the hospital bed in hushed silence. With the four of them, the room was crowded. Nick, Stephen, and Miriam pushed close to the bed. Kiki hung back. Tears rolled down Miriam's cheeks. Stephen had been there since early afternoon, and the strain showed in his face. Nick leaned close, looking for a response from the slack face of his father.

Kiki felt badly for Nick. He had seen so little of his family the last four years. He had visited home on only two of his leaves from his medic assignment in Afghanistan. During his last visit, his family asked him to stay and go back to medical school. He stayed for a while, but re-upped and returned to Afghanistan.

If he hadn't done that, she would never have met him, Kiki thought.

The last two years they had only communicated with his family via the shortwave from the boat. Only a few sentences were exchanged on each call. It was a risk for them to return to the United States. If the FBI learned they were still alive, the pursuit would start.

Kiki looked at the life monitor. Doctor Michael Sabino lay unmoving. His heartbeat was steady, blood pressure low, probably due to the drugs. His chest barely moved as he breathed. She had to leave.

In the hallway, she leaned against the wall. Watching Nick's family brought up memories of her family. There had never been a moment like this. Kiki was on assignment, away, and they were murdered because of her. She never got to say goodbye. A sob heaved out of her chest.

Nick found her in the small lobby. "Are you okay?"

"Watching you with your family was a scene I'll never have. It hurts."

Nick sat, putting his arm around her. "Is there anything I can do?"

"Just hold me. Tell me what's happening with your father." That'll take my mind away from my own, she thought.

"The doctor came in after you left. The CAT scan showed a lot of damage. They want to put in a shunt to keep the fluid from building up. Mom has to give permission. Without it, he'll die."

"What's his prognosis afterward?"

"The doctor gave some rosy projections, but the reality is he won't recover enough to be more than an invalid. Whatever Mom decides, Stephen and I will support her. She needs to decide by tomorrow."

"Wow."

"Yeah. She's exhausted, but wants to stay with him. We're going to take her home and come back in the morning. Stephen's going home, too. He needs to be with Barbara and the kids for a little while. There's nothing we can do here, and Dad won't wake up tonight."

The short ride home was quiet, everyone lost in thought. A few lights were on in the house, either on timers or photocells. Miriam said, "I'm going to make some tea. Do you want some?"

"I'll have some with you, Mom," said Nick.

Kiki squeezed Nick's hand. "I'm really tired. I'm going to bed." Kiki thought her presence would be an intrusion. "Goodnight, Miriam. See you tomorrow." She needed some alone-time. Hours later, she was still awake when Nick came to bed.

"Nick," her voice caught, "I'm going to take a drive to visit my parents' ranch tomorrow." She added in a whisper, "I need to do that."

"I can't go with you. I have to stay with Mom. She wasn't firm on a decision, but Dad didn't believe in just keeping people alive. He always thought death was as much a part of life as breathing."

Nick sighed. "But she has to be ready to let him go."

Kiki reached out and pulled Nick close. "And you? What about you?"

"I wish I could say I was fine, but I'm not. A lot of pain and guilt is piling up."

She hugged him tightly. "I know. I've got ghosts chasing me, too. I have to go to the ranch – try to put them to rest. I have to do it alone. Knowing you'll be here when I return is the only thing giving me the courage to do this."

"It's the same for me, K. Without you, I'm not sure I could handle coming back, Mom, Dad, this...."

They clung together, each acting as a life raft for the other. She comforted him as he comforted her. Sleep came, but not good sleep.

Images of Kiki's family kept calling. She heard Nick crying in his sleep.

Chapter Four

September 10
Marana, Arizona

Kiki exited the interstate at Marana and headed west. Little had changed since her last visit over two years ago. The morning sun was at her back, casting long shadows. The air was crisp and clear. After twenty minutes, she left the maintained dirt road, turning onto the track to her parents' ranch. Their dented mailbox sat at an angle, the door open, gaping like a baby's mouth waiting for the next bite. After their death, she'd arranged to have the taxes paid and the livestock sold. The road was overgrown, washed out in places. As she neared the ranch house, her stomach fluttered. She tamped down her unease.

Weeds nearly obscured the house. The adobe walls were cracked and windows broken. The place was a wreck. The ash tree they'd planted to shade the house was dead, as was the eucalyptus, plaintiff branches reaching toward the sky for water that didn't come. Kiki turned off the engine and sat. The last time she'd been here, the house was surrounded by yellow crime scene tape. Traces of it still hung from the bushes in the still morning air.

As she got out of the SUV, she heard quail calling, cackling as they scrounged for breakfast, went for a drink. It was a familiar sound that brought a fleeting smile to her lips. The porch roof sagged, the love seat swing hung from only one chain. Kiki opened the door with a screech of protesting hinges.

It was dim inside. Trash littered the floor, leaves were piled in corners by the wind. The room smelled of rot. The furniture was broken, cushions ripped and stuffing strewn about like dirty snow. The place had been used by smugglers, but not for a long time. The kitchen was bare. The stove and refrigerator were gone, stolen. The sink had been ripped out, too. As she stood, her mind filled in the missing pieces, repaired the broken furniture and cabinets, mended the cracked floor and broken window until she saw her mother's kitchen again. It was her mother's kitchen, not hers. Never hers.

Down the hall, she stopped in front of her parents' closed door. Kiki couldn't bring herself to open it. That would be an invasion. The room she had shared with her husband, Chet, was open. Through the doorway she saw the collapsed bed, mattress on the floor. There were holes in the walls. It smelled like death – or was that her imagination.

At her daughter's room, she broke down, collapsing into a heap on the filthy floor. A rag against the wall of the bedroom looked like one of Lindy's dresses. Kiki held it as sobs wracked her slender frame.

She had left her family to go fight in a foreign land, and the enemy had come here. They had struck a blow more devastating than any wound she suffered in Afghanistan. Katherine Russell, named the Iblis by her enemies, had taken her revenge. But it didn't bring her family back.

The sunlight moved across the floor, unseen. Her mind, nearly frozen, allowed the pain in by dribs and drabs so it wouldn't overwhelm her. She had to forgive herself for abandoning them to savages.

There was no use wondering what ifs. She had served her country, and while she was gone... "I'm sorry," she whispered to the ghosts. "If only I hadn't gone."

You wouldn't have met Nick.

Guilt arose. She had loved Chet, but not like she loved Nick. Life with Chet on the ranch had been safe and secure, but she could not have lived that life. It wasn't in her. Chet, her mom and her dad saw this, but Lindy was too young to understand. Her five-year old mind only saw her mom leaving.

Kiki cried from the depths of her soul against the unfairness of life. When she finally returned, shadows had crept across the floor. The sun was sinking into the west.

At the front door, she turned and looked one last time into the house. The hinges creaked as she closed the door on that life and strode to the SUV. The past was done.

She had a new life to build.

Chapter Five

September 10
Casa Grande, Arizona

"Dad, can you hear me?" Nick looked at the man in the bed, a mere shadow. "Dad, it's Nick." The monitors in the background beeped as they traced heart rate and respiration. Neither was strong. His dad's eyes fluttered and focused on Nick. A faint smile crossed his lips. Nick reached out, putting a hand on his shoulder. Dad nodded, closed his eyes. The monitors went flat, alarms sounded.

Two nurses rushed in, pushing Nick aside. One began CPR, the other ran for the defib. Nick watched them, but he knew it was Dad's time. He'd waited for Nick, to see him once more before going.

Miriam and Stephen arrived fifteen minutes later. His mother was in shock. "They said I had more time," she wailed.

Nick took her in his arms. "Dad was waiting for me, Mom. He said goodbye to you and Stephen, and he waited for me."

The family hugged each other, all crying. The pale husk that was his father lay still. Nick was the first to leave the room. In the hall, he leaned against the wall, tears freely flowing. Why had he gone off to a foreign land? Why had he left? Why didn't he go to medical school? The questions poured in, his mind unable to process them, unable to stop them. The trip back to the house was lost in a blur.

There was some magic network that alerted everybody that Doctor Sabino had passed. Within hours of their arrival at home, calls started. Patients, former patients, friends and colleagues offered condolences and help. Nick, Barbara and Stephen answered the phones, thanking callers for their concerns, assuring them that if any help were needed they'd call. By midnight they needed a break and turned the phones off.

It was pleasant out by the pool. The kids were inside watching TV, playing games. The adults were thankful for the peace. The visiting well-wishers had been sent home, their Velveetta-laden casseroles on the counter. Nobody was hungry.

Stephen looked from Nick to Kiki. "Nick, why weren't you here?" he asked with an accusatory tone.

Miriam held up a hand, "There's no room here for recriminations. But, Nick, we want to know what happened in Afghanistan, and after. We knew you were there as a medic. We didn't know you'd left the Army for God's sake, until the FBI contacted us. Where have you been? What did you do?"

"Nick, what was that letter you sent us?" Stephen asked. "You know the one telling us not to open it, to send it to Fox News if we didn't hear from you? Dad, Mom and I were worried sick."

Nick looked from Stephen to his mom. He owed them an answer. Kiki gave him a nod.

Kiki spoke up. "Mrs. Sabino, Stephen, it's because of me. When I came home to our ranch in Marana after the murder of my family...,"

"Russell! Your last name is Russell! Was your family massacred south of here a few years ago?" asked Stephen, his eyes wide.

Mrs. Sabino's hand flew to her mouth.

Kiki nodded. "I needed help and reached out to Nick. He came."

"But they solved those murders," exclaimed Stephen. "I read it in the papers, saw it on CNN."

"They did," responded Nick. "We helped. We helped them afterward, too."

"That's where we got into trouble," said Kiki, staring from Mrs. Sabino to Stephen. "We worked with other government agencies fighting terrorism and got caught in a squabble between them. We had to disappear."

Mrs. Sabino's face showed her puzzlement.

"Mom, they wanted us to do things that were wrong," explained Nick, holding his hands out. "They threatened us with jail if we didn't cooperate."

"Our government wouldn't do that," she muttered, shaking her head.

"Mom, we had to disappear. Our return to the United States may still be a danger."

"Even a danger to you and Stephen," added Kiki. "We don't know for sure. They believe we're dead. If we pop up on their radar, we're not sure what will happen, but the chances are nothing good."

"We don't want to take any chances, so nobody but the family knows we're here," said

Nick. He watched his mom to see how she took this story. She'd watched enough crime drama thrillers that she understood, but the reality had not worked in.

Stephen rose. "It's really late. I need to get Barbara and the kids home. I'll tell her to say nothing about you and Kiki, but she'll demand to know why. We'll come over tomorrow to help get things done, services arrangements and all that." He kissed Miriam on the cheek, hugged Nick. "Whatever happened, it's good to have you back. Kiki, it's a pleasure to meet you. Too bad it's under these circumstances."

Kiki watched him go into the house to round up the kids and hustle them to the car. Nick walked them to the door.

Miriam looked at her. "Whatever trouble you and Nick are in, I'm glad you are with him. It's obvious to me you are his world. Take care of him."

Kiki watched her walk inside, shoulders straight, head high. She was a strong woman, one to admire.

Chapter Six

September 11
North Korea

The room was dim, lit by glowing computer screens. The North Korean Military Technology Center was a hive of activity, with people hunched over their workstations. Lieutenant Gun Rahn looked intently over the shoulder of Sergeant Kwang Ryang. His computer was scrolling through the last list of password tries to get past the firewall and into the electrical grid control system for the eastern sector of the United States.

His team had been working on this particular firewall for months. Once they were into this system, they could disrupt the electrical power distribution for the whole eastern seaboard.

Gun didn't know how many teams were working on other sectors, but he knew there were many. The Supreme Leader had ordered an all-out cyber attack on the United States. It was about to pay off, and on the anniversary of the greatest successful attack on American soil, September 11.

His heart swelled. His country, the Democratic People's Republic of Korea, was going to strike one of the greatest blows against the imperialist giant, the United States. Not only was the power grid soon to be in their control, but the communications, water and gas distribution systems and the internet.

Attacks on the banking systems had already disrupted commerce. These had been going on for years. After each attack, the system would find how to block the attack. And the DPRK learned what to do to strike again.

The unsuccessful attack on the New York dam spillway by Iran had been a test, one to learn the system and the defenses. It had failed because a single valve was offline. They shared their expertise. This time, the attack would be successful.

This was going to be a carefully coordinated series of attacks. The disruption to America would be greater than if a nuclear bomb had gone off. A bomb only struck in one small area. This would be all across America. True, the psychological effect of a nuclear bomb would be greater, but only for a while. Shivering in the dark with no help coming was much worse. The attacks were against civilian targets, not military. The civilian targets were much softer. These attacks would put pressure on the government and the military from the people. It would be much harder to trace the source from civilian targets.

"We're in!" exclaimed Sergeant Ryang. A schematic of the electrical grid for New York appeared on his screen. "What are your orders, Lieutenant?"

"The transformers for New York City, distribution center" Gun said pointing at the symbols, "are the first target. Our shooters are targeting those transformers. Turn on the overrides. Block out other controls. Load and unload it in one-minute intervals. Monitor the transformer temperatures. Bypass the safety shutdowns. When it overheats and goes offline, go to this one," he said pointing at another. Repeat this until all the transformers center are down."

Gun watched the schematic of the control center. Power lines went from green to yellow to red, then back to green. The cycle repeated. One of the transformer icons changed from green to yellow, signaling it was overheating. He pointed at it. "That's one we hit. Override the shutdown." The transformer icon changed to red then blinked off. Other icons began to flash.

Gun nodded. This was only one distribution center, the first. The power company would be moving to bypass the ruined transformers, the outage would be short-lived. Meanwhile, Gun directed Ryang to another distribution center near Washington, D.C.

The power companies would begin investigations as to why the transformers failed. They would find the bullet holes draining the coolant. They would then investigate why the shutdowns failed. Their redundant systems would be eventually overwhelmed. Parts of New York City would only experience a few hours outage. It would be the same for Washington, D.C. This was not just an attack. It was a siege. They would go dark for a long time

Replacements for the burned-up transformers were available in very limited quantities. The lead-time for new ones was from months to over a year. As soon as the warehouse stocks were depleted, the lights would stay off. The American public was about to realize they were at war, and they were the targets. This war wasn't about killing the enemy. It was destroying their economy and infrastructure.

Chapter Seven

September 11
Center for Disease Control
Atlanta, Georgia

Dr. Joel Albertson, Director of the Center for Disease Control, glanced nervously around the conference table and at the multiple monitors with those teleconferencing into the meeting. "Ladies and gentlemen, thank you for attending. I'm sorry this meeting was called on a weekend, but as you will see, we have a potential emergency. Most of you have not heard, but we are receiving reports of smallpox cases." He watched those physically present glance at each other. Those attending via teleconference frowned. "As of one hour ago, we have more than one-thousand deaths reported and several thousand cases. We are seeing a very high percentage of hemorrhagic smallpox rather than the historical two percent. This is extremely troubling, as the hemorrhagic is almost always fatal."

"Impossible! This disease was eradicated years ago!" exclaimed Doctor Goldstein.

"Ishmael, please let me continue. There will be time for comments and questions in a few minutes. You are correct. We thought it was wiped out. There are numerous things about this outbreak that are most disturbing. First, the cases are in many locations, mostly big cities. Second, those with the disease recently returned from foreign countries, different foreign countries."

Everyone started speaking at once. Joel waited a minute before rapping on the table and calling for silence. "We are trying to quarantine those showing symptoms and trying to track down everyone on those flights. It is proving exceptionally difficult. Many of those passengers met connecting flights from the international airports where they arrived. If we don't get control of this quickly, this could become our worst case nightmare."

He looked at the shocked faces. Ishmael spoke up, voicing the rising concern. "A dead disease, multiple departure cities, multiple destination cities. This is not happening by accident." He looked at those around the table.

Joel's voice broke the dead silence. "A bio-attack is a very real possibility. This information must be kept confidential. Panic will create a disaster. I will appoint several of you to different committees. We need a coordinated containment and quarantine committee. We need to begin vaccine manufacture. We need to investigate how this extinct virus is now out into the public sector." He glanced at those attending.

"Doctor Ayres is reviewing qualifications and will assign personnel to those committees. I must begin drafting a report to the president. The details of...." The monitors with those teleconferencing went blank.

Then the lights went out.

Chapter Eight

September 11
Casa Grande, Arizona

After the late night, Kiki and Nick woke at mid-morning to the smell of coffee wafting down from the kitchen. Nick donned a robe and wandered out. Kiki headed for the shower.

"Mom, did you get any sleep?" asked Nick, filling his cup from the coffee machine.

"No," was all she said.

"What do you need? How can we help?"

"I called Jacob at the funeral home and made arrangements to have a memorial service. Michael wanted his body to go the University of Arizona Medical School for teaching purposes. I've called them. I've called the paper, but I'll need help writing the obituary. Michael started writing one last year. We talked about this day, but it was always 'someday in the future.' The reality of it never existed before."

Nick went to his mom and held her. She buried her head in his chest. "Together we made out a task list." Tears streaked her cheeks. "What am I going to do with myself, Nick? What am I going to do without Michael?" she wailed.

His strong mother seems so frail at that moment. "We're here together, Mom. We'll get through this. Do you want me to put a message on the phone that we aren't accepting calls or visitors for a while?"

"No. One thing your dad believed was that we must understand things through another's eyes. The people calling need to express their condolences and offer sympathy. They'll help me get through the grieving."

Any idea of keeping his and Kiki's return quiet was now out of the question. They had to come up with a story. "I'll call Stephen. His family will want to be here."

Miriam nodded. "Can you fix breakfast, or lunch or whatever? I'm not really hungry, but we need to eat."

"I can do that," said Kiki, entering the kitchen. The phone rang. It was the first call of many. "Miriam, you sit down and man the phone while you can. Nick can take over in an hour."

With Nick's help, Kiki found what she needed to make a sausage, egg, and cheese skillet with toast and hash browns. Miriam chose to eat while answering the phone. Stephen came in. "Mom, how are you?"

She waved to him, the phone to her ear. "Instead of flowers, we'd like contributions in Michael's name made to his favorite charities, Planned Parenthood, Habitat for Humanity, Casa de Los Niños, or the Food Bank."

"Is she okay?" Stephen asked, nodding toward his mother.

"We're going to man the phone in shifts to give her a break," said Kiki.

Stephen took a bite of the scrambled eggs. "Barb and the kids will be over later. She's running the restaurant while the kids are in school. People are going to start coming over soon."

"I know," said Nick. "They'll being ten times the amount of food we can eat. Mom decided we could take everything that's left to the rescue kitchen later."

"That's a nice idea," said Kiki from the sink, cleaning up the dishes from breakfast.

"We've been taking food from the restaurant over there at the end of each day," said

Stephen. "Some of those people are eating gourmet. It makes us feel good to help."

Kiki regarded Nick and Stephen, then Miriam. This was a special family she had married into. Nick was unique, but now she understood it came from an empathic family life.

The doorbell rang. The start of the parade of well-wishers and sympathizers had begun. Kiki motioned to Miriam to go to the door. "I'll take over here for you. Go ahead and meet your friends." After several questions about services for Michael, she made a command decision, telling people that the Celebration of Life service and reception would be held at Stephen's restaurant, Cocina de Sabino, date and time to be announced.

As the day wore on, the cheese and vegetable platters, casseroles, cakes and pies piled up on the table. Vases of flowers sat on every available surface. Stephen manned the bar on the patio.

If this was just well-wishers, what would the Celebration of Life service be like, wondered Kiki.

Stephen's wife and the two kids arrived at four-thirty. Barb took over the phone, giving Kiki a needed break. After a search for Nick, she took his arm and led him to their bedroom.

"Nick, how are you holding up?"

"I'm coping. We haven't been around this many people in a long time."

"Years," agreed Kiki.

"Stephen wanted me to express thanks for your decision to have the Celebration of Life service at the restaurant. Good call. Let's go out on the patio with the family. The guests should have left by now."

The guests had indeed gone. Barb was puttering about, picking up here and there, putting perishables in the refrigerator. Miriam and Stephen were sitting on the patio, glasses of wine in hand.

Nick handed Kiki a glass, and they joined them. Miriam and Stephen smiled as they sat. Silently, they looked out at the twinkling lights of the city below. It was the way Nick remembered from years before, so peaceful, so normal,

Chapter Nine

September 11
Casa Grande, Arizona

Stephen's son came out. "Dad, Sheriff Tierman's here."

Nick stood as the uniformed man came through the door. They studied each other for a moment then hugged, slapping each other on the back. The six foot-three inch Brad Tierman, his high school friend, was fit and trim, like the linebacker he had been in high school.

Nick stepped back. "What's with the bald head?"

"It's easier to take care of with the helmets and hats we wear in this heat." He ran his hand across his head and turned toward Miriam. "I'm sorry I couldn't get by earlier to see you. Things were pretty crazy yesterday. We've been getting reports of rolling blackouts in other parts of the country. We're on watch ourselves." He smiled at Nick. "You've been in the sun a lot yourself."

"Brad, I'd like you to meet my–"

"I'm Katherine Russell," she said, rising to shake his hand.

Brad paused half-a-beat before offering his hand. "Brad Tierman. Pleased to meet you." He looked at her intently.

Did he know who she was? Did he know about her family? "Yes, Sheriff, I'm that Katherine Russell." Her eyes held his.

"Brad, have a seat. You want a beer?" asked Nick.

He glanced at Nick. "Can't. On call. I will take a glass of ice water." His eyes returned to Kiki. "Call me Brad. Katherine, I was going to ask how you corralled Nick."

Kiki laughed. "Oops, TMI, Call me Kiki". She watched the calculating going on behind Brad's eyes, processing the new information.

"I'll get your water," said Stephen. "Mom could use another wine, and I need to check on the kids."

Miriam watched Brad and Nick, assessing. "Brad, is there any reason Kiki and Nick should be worried?" she asked.

Brad broke eye contact with Kiki.

"No, ma'am. We had an inquiry about Katherine almost two years ago. It was just a request for any records we had. We had none. Another request came through about Nick a month later. All of his misdeeds, just prank stuff we did together as kids, were in his youth, and those records don't exist anymore."

Kiki let out a breath she didn't know she was holding. Didn't have or didn't send? she wondered. There was a strange dynamic going on between Nick and Brad.

Brad turned to her. "There have been rumors about both of you. One is that you saved a cop's life. Another is that you took care of those who killed your family. Good stories that go around the table at the bar. Whether true or not, my hat's off to you." He held up his glass in a mock toast. "I'd like to hear your version sometime. How long are you here?" he asked Nick.

"As long as we're needed," Nick said, watching his mother. "We haven't talked about it yet." Miriam stared back, waiting for more. She wanted to know, too.

Stephen returned, handing Brad a tall glass of ice water. He set his mom's wine in front of her. Startled at first, she took a sip.

Stephen glanced at the faces. "What did I miss?"

"Brad, are you my friend first or a lawman first?"

Brad stared at him. "Don't tell me anything I shouldn't know and I won't have to make that decision."

"Okay, here's the PG rated version," said Nick. "Kiki was the hottest sniper in Afghanistan, highest number of kills, second highest in the Middle East." Brad smiled at Kiki. She watched him telling the story. "She was really hurting them, so the ragheads put a price on her head. One of the local chieftains wanted to collect. He set up an ambush that nearly worked. When it didn't succeed, they sent a team to the U.S. to kill her family. After that killing, they began a program to kill the dependents of those serving in Afghanistan." Brad's eyes were locked on Nick.

"Kiki came back for the services for her family. The sheriff had assumed the killing was smugglers, the case was at a dead end. She asked me to help her track down her family's murderers, so I returned. We helped the FBI find the killers."

A troubled expression passed over Brad's face. "I never heard anything about a trial." Neither Nick nor Kiki said anything.

Nick continued, "We were working with the FBI and the CIA. When a disagreement broke out about our services, we had to disappear."

Kiki knew Brad was full of questions, wanting details, but he said nothing.

Kiki spoke up, "At this point, the government believes we are dead. It would be best for them to continue in that belief." She understood that this put Brad in an uncomfortable position. If an official inquiry came asking about them, he would have to lie, or not.

Brad's radio crackled. He put it to his ear. "I'm leaving now," he spoke into it as he stood. "I have to go. A big power outage hit us. My condolences, Mrs. Sabino, Stephen, Nick. It was a pleasure meeting you, Katherine. Maybe we'll see each other again."

As he turned toward the door, Stephen's son appeared. "Dad, something's wrong with the TV."

"Lucky you're on solar," said Brad. "Sounds like most of the town's out." He left, hurrying toward the front door.

Stephen rose. "I'll walk you out. I should probably call the restaurant to see what's happening there."

"Nick, what are your plans?" asked his mother.

Nick looked at Kiki. "Once upon a time, I wanted to come back here, go to med school, and take over Dad's practice. Now, I don't know. Kiki and I have danced around the subject of a long-term future. This trip has brought a number of questions up. We could idle a lot of days away aboard our boat, but that life was getting old."

Kiki spoke, "We talked about the future the last few months. The problem is that Nick and I are listed as dead. We've done nothing to change that assumption by members of our government. If they found out that wasn't the case, we might be in trouble."

"Mom, we just don't know. We don't even know how to find out."

"Do you think Bradley could help?" she asked, tilting her head to one side.

"Mrs. Sabino, anybody checking on us might be like peering into a hornets' nest to see if they're mad," said Kiki.

Stephen came out. "Looks like the cell phone system is out. Mom, your house kicked into isolation mode for the night – small appliances, lights, refrigerator and freezer only, until power comes back on or the sun comes up. I need to get to the restaurant. Things are probably a mess. Nick, Kiki, see you tomorrow." He leaned down and kissed his mom's cheek.

Chapter Ten

September 12
Washington, D.C.

"How widespread are the power outages?" asked President Donaldson. He viewed the faces of the assembled Cabinet. His Secretary of the Interior, Ron Carson pressed a button on his tablet. The president liked Carson. He was bright, young, and not afraid to kick ass. His youthful appearance, dark hair and strong jaw didn't hurt his chances in politics.

Carson looked up. "The power outages started along the east coast." The large screen on the wall showed the eastern United States. Washington, D.C. New York, Philadelphia, and Atlanta were circled in red. "Some grids are back on, but then others kick out. We are now getting reports of outages on the west coast."

The map changed to California, Oregon and Washington. Los Angeles, San Diego, San Francisco, Portland and Seattle were circled in red.

"Mr. President, somebody shot the transformers in our large stations. When the cooling oil drained out, they burned up because the shutdowns failed. Our control systems were hacked. This is a double attack on our electrical grid. A cyber attack disabled the protection. When the transformers lost the cooling, they toasted. The latest reports indicate that across the country we've lost some generating plants, too, mostly coal or gas. We lost some hydropower when the controls for the turbines cut out and they over-spun. We were lucky there were only minor injuries, but those turbines were a loss. The nuclear plants are more secure. The real problem is the transformer stations and the distribution systems are dropping offline. The bypasses haven't worked because these attacks have been at key points in the grid. Isolating the control systems has not totally solved the problems. This virus disabling the safety and control systems may be buried in our hardware."

"General Edwards, are you aware of this?" asked the president.

"Mr. President, it is an attack. We're trying to track down the shooters and the source or sources of the cyber attack now. If this virus is buried in the hardware, this has been planned for a long time. It won't be a quick fix."

"Mr. President," Ron spoke up. "The problem is the components that have failed or may fail are long lead-time items. Our warehouse stocks of transformers, switchgear, control systems, and turbines will not cover the losses if this continues much longer."

The president turned toward General Edwards. "Sounds like you're under the gun, Tom. He turned to Ron. Let's get the pipeline opened up for replacements. What's our source?"

"China," said Ron. "The last of our domestic suppliers stopped making parts last year. They couldn't compete. We're searching other stocks from friendly nations, like Canada."

"Americans won't tolerate being in the dark for long," muttered the president.

"Sir," started Ron, "that's not all. With the loss of power, we've also lost cell phone towers, limiting service in many areas."

"Okay, let's cut to the chase," snapped the president. "How soon can we restore services?"

Ron shook his head. "We're working on getting those estimates to you now. We're also prioritizing where our efforts should go. I'll have that list later today for your approval."

"General, do we need to call out the National Guard?" asked the president. "I don't want to wait until the riots start."

"Their presence may lend some assurance that we are working to solve this quickly. We can bring in supplies and generator systems for the hospitals and local law enforcement."

"Mr. President," said Ron, "let's contact the governors, let them know what we want to do. I'm sure they'll agree to this plan. Start the mobilization. Without cell service, it won't happen as fast as we'd like. In the meantime, we'll focus on getting communications back up."

The president nodded.

There was a knock at the door. "Mr. President, I have an urgent message from the Director of the Center for Disease Control. He's been unable to reach you, so he sent a courier." The president motioned for the courier to enter. A woman stepped into the office. She was tall and slender with short frosted hair.

"Mr. President, I'm Dr. Adriana Getzwiller from the CDC. We've been trying to get a message to you since yesterday. Our power and communication systems are down. Our emergency generators are carrying our power needs for now, but communications are out."

"We're aware of outages. What is so critical that the CDC had to send you?"

"We were getting reports of smallpox outbreaks before the loss of communications." She approached the table and handed the president a file folder. "These are the last reports we received. Outbreaks have occurred in several sites across the country – simultaneously." That word hung in the silence of the room.

"What's the CDC doing about these occurrences right now?" asked the president.

"Sir, we're preparing quarantine protocols."

The president turned to Carson. "Get me a secure radio link to the CDC." He turned to General Edwards, "Include biohazard procedures in your alert for the National Guard. Start drawing up plans to bring in the Army."

The president held up a hand to forestall the general's objection. "I know I can't use the Army domestically except in the case of national emergency. This may be one." He turned to his Chief of Staff, William Jackman. "Bill, I need an emergency session of Congress. Start working on my speech. Whether they object to our plans or not, this is beyond politics. We have to inform them of what's happening. In no uncertain terms, the United States is under attack."

Chapter Eleven

September 13
Casa Grande, Arizona

Nick and Stephen dollied the cartons of frozen food from the truck through the service entrance into the bottom level under the house. The cool darkness was welcome relief from the afternoon heat.

"Thanks for the help, Nick. With power still out, things in the freezers at the restaurant would start thawing soon. We may be premature and have to move it back this afternoon, but nobody knows when power will be restored."

Nick nodded as they stacked cartons in one of his mother's walk-in freezers. Dad had put in two, with heavy insulation and being in constant seventy-five degrees underground, they would operate off the solar system. "I'll try to reach

Brad when we're done to see if I can find out anything."

When the last cartons were stashed, they took the elevator up to the kitchen. "Mom, thanks for letting us store the food here. Things were starting to thaw. We'd lose everything by tonight. By the time insurance came through, we'd be out of business."

"Glad we could help." She smiled at him as he kissed her on the cheek.

"I'm going to give Brad a call, see what he knows," said Nick. He walked to the phone. The landlines still worked.

"Mom, has there been anything on TV or the internet?" Stephen asked.

"The TV's snow, and the internet has a lot of crazy stuff about an attack and an invasion. The radio is broadcasting about an emergency, telling us to stay tuned. They are saying this is a temporary situation and stay calm."

Nick walked over. "Brad could only talk to me for a few seconds. The power is out for the whole valley. Only those with emergency generators, like the Sheriff's Department and the hospital are running. Reports from Phoenix are the same. Without power, water distribution is out except for the gas driven pumps. The governor told him to prepare for help from the National Guard."

"That sounds serious," exclaimed Stephen, "and long term."

Nick looked at him. The enormity of long-term outages was sinking in. "Maybe we should move other things from the restaurant up here," he said.

"Surely, it won't be that bad," said his mother.

"It won't hurt," said Stephen, nodding. "Mom, can I bring Barb and the kids up too?"

"You know you can," Miriam said, in a light tone, "but this will be over in a few hours. Won't we feel foolish?" She smiled.

Stephen went to the landline and called Barb.

"Better foolish than any alternative I can think of," said Nick. He and Stephen headed back down to the truck.

"Powerless for a couple of days would be bad, but without water, people start to die. They won't put up with that. I suspect that's the reason for the National Guard." said Nick as they walked.

Stephen frowned at Nick. "Surely the guard will bring in critical supplies. How could this happen?"

"The message behind the message is this may be an attack, a cyber attack." Nick stared at Stephen. "If Phoenix is affected, I'd bet other large metro areas are too. It could overwhelm our ability to fix it quickly if this is widespread enough," he mused aloud. "Let's bring your shortwave back. We may get better information from it."

Stephen nodded. "A lot of the guys I talk to regularly have their own generators. We should be able to hear something."

The streets were deserted as they drove into town. The radio instructed people to go to the schools for emergency water supplies. Once loaded with things from the restaurant, they headed for Stephen's house.

With solar cells, there was enough power to operate fans, but not the air conditioning. Without water, the evaporative cooling was out, too. The house was well insulated, so it wasn't intolerable, yet.

Barb was in the kitchen filling ice chests from the freezer and refrigerator. The kids had their suitcases ready. Stephen got his shortwave radio. "We'll need an antenna," he said. "I've got an old one in the garage. If we put it on top of the mountain, we should be able to reach about anywhere." Nick and Barb started loading the things into the truck. Stephen came out with the antenna and coils of wire. Barb went in to get the kids and for a last check. The house looked deserted as they left, Barb following in her SUV. He wondered what they'd come back to.

Chapter Twelve

September 14
Washington, D.C.

The president looked around the table at his cabinet. The faces were serious. This was a crisis meeting. The topics were the smallpox outbreak and the cyber attack that was paralyzing much of the nation. "Gentlemen and ladies, after my meeting with Congress, I've asked Speaker of the House, Elizabeth Gutierrez and Senator Robert Chou to sit in." He nodded to them. "We will hear about the smallpox outbreaks first." On a wall monitor was Dr. Albertson, Director of the CDC. "Dr. Albertson, what's the latest on the smallpox occurrences?"

The face of the doctor stared at them with reddened eyes. He was obviously under great stress. "Mr. President, the loss of communications has made the assessment difficult. The internet has been our only tool. We've had reports of outbreaks in the major airport hubs with international terminals. With a two-week gestation period, we started looking for something that happened last month. We got lucky.

"On a flight into Seattle last month, a man gave a bubble toy to a child. The flight attendant took it from the child as it was annoying other passengers, offering to return it after landing. The family deplaned before she could give it back, so she turned it in to lost and found. When the child and the flight attendant both came down with smallpox, she remembered the bubble toy. Our lab in Seattle is checking it now."

There were shocked faces around the table.

"Mr. President," said Albertson, "this is looking like a bio-attack."

"Jesus Christ!" exclaimed the president. "They're using children. A bio-attack is bad, but using children as the carriers. Who are these monsters?"

FBI Director Athena Brown spoke up, "Mr. President, Dr. Albertson has kept us in the loop." She turned her brown eyes to the monitor and nodded at the doctor. "We checked video records of the immigration area where we spotted a man giving a bubble toy to another child. We are doing the same on other international flights. In addition, we are trying to use facial recognition to follow this man. He appears again at a Seattle Seahawks football game with another bubble toy.

"In checking the passenger manifest for flights arriving at the time, he appears in the immigration area, his passport identifies him as Victor Pushkin. He stayed at the Courtyard Downtown but has since checked out. We are looking for him now at the highest priority.

"With this information, we began checking other flights arriving at the cities with outbreaks. Men with bubble toys show up at each. We have their names and have all-points-bulletins out for them. Perhaps the most insidious attack was by Anatoly Tsaryov who went to Disneyland. We have video of him giving children bubble toys.

"Sir," said Athena, her normally pleasant face twisted with anger, "we will catch these bastards. In the meantime, we have begun background checks based on the names we have. Each is a Russian citizen, though we are trying to make sure those were valid names on the passports."

"Have you asked the Russian Embassy for help?" asked Secretary of State Sharon Volgyi.

"We have not. At this point, we don't know if the government is involved or if this is some splinter group. What we have done is set up a cordon around the Russian Embassies. If these bastards are sanctioned, they will not get into the embassy for asylum. If they try to claim diplomatic immunity, only our guards will hear it as they are whisked off. We need to interrogate them to investigate this."

"Is there any reason to believe this might be sanctioned?" asked the president.

General Edwards tapped on a tablet. "Sir, I'm sending out a little history of smallpox. It is pertinent. If you follow along, I'll summarize." He took a deep breath. "Smallpox is a disease that has been with us for centuries," he began. "It has killed millions in that time. Smallpox was used as a bio-weapon by the British in the French and Indian Wars. In another incident of smallpox as a weapon, it is suspected the British used it in New South Wales against the native population." He glanced up to shaking heads and troubled expressions.

"During World War II, the United Kingdom, the United States, and Japan tried to weaponize smallpox. Those plans were dropped due to the widespread availability of vaccines."

"The U.S. participated in developing a bio weapon?" asked the president.

"Yes, sir. In 1947, the Soviet Union established a smallpox weapons factory in Zagorsk. They developed extremely powerful strains that nearly got away from them, killing a number of citizens before being brought under control. After decades of development and allegations of tons of stored bioweapons, the Russian government announced that all remaining stores would be moved to the Vector Institute in Koltsovo. With the breakup of the Soviet Union, there are fears that those stockpiles may have fallen into other hands."

Edwards continued. "One of our greatest fears is that genetically modified strains resistant to our vaccines may have been developed. With calls for the eradication of all stores, the vaccine programs have all but ceased. Obviously, obliteration of smallpox has not occurred. Sir, the world is vulnerable to a global epidemic that could kill millions."

"Thank you, Tom. That paints a bleak picture." The room was silent. The president looked at the monitor. "Doctor, what are your plans to combat these outbreaks?"

"Mr. President, we started a series of public announcements telling those who suspect they have contracted the disease to seek medical aid immediately. We are initiating a vaccine-manufacturing program. We are moving ahead with an aggressive program of quarantine in areas of infection, but frankly, sir we will need federal help to enforce any large-scale quarantine. The key to any success is to move rapidly."

"My God!" exclaimed Secretary of the Interior, Ron Carson. "We're talking about shutting down the United States. We might have to isolate cities like New York and Los Angeles. Everything would grind to a halt. The losses would be staggering."

"Mr. Secretary," said Albertson, "the losses will be staggering when millions of our citizens die. The United States may well be quarantined by other nations in the world, enforced by the navies of our allies and enemies alike. If we err on the side of over-aggression, the losses will be small in comparison."

"This is massive," said the president, shaking his head. "It's not the only attack we are facing. Secretary Ron Carson has been following the cyber attack that has shut down the power distribution system."

Ron glanced at the cabinet members, the president, and the members of congress. More bad news, he thought. "As most of you are aware, our electric grid suffered a cyber attack shutting down power to many areas of our country. Utilities have been working overtime to restore those systems. The attack has damaged equipment with long lead-times for replacements. We are exploring every avenue to replace damaged equipment and protect our systems. In short, we are forced to prioritize our efforts and resources. There are areas that will not have power restored in the near term. We will have to deploy assets and people to prevent disaster.

"If we allow it, this could turn into a huge political battle. We cannot let that happen. I do not believe the goal of these attacks is to kill people, though that will certainly happen. I believe these attacks are aimed at destroying the economy of the United States. Our people are the tools in this battle."

The president looked hard at Carson. "Ron, thank you. You've seen past the carnage and divined a purpose. You are correct about the looming political battles as to who and where assets will be directed and we must put Congress on notice that this must not happen. The larger picture must dominate. This is a war for the survival of the United States.:

Carson flushed momentarily at the praise then continued. "It would appear that these attacks are coordinated. That raises the question of who is behind it?"

"Thank you, Secretary Carson. What is apparent to me is that we must respond immediately. Whether we address the bio-attack or the cyber attack first, we're going to need troops on the ground. I have instructed the governors to mobilize the National Guard, and I will deploy the military within the borders of the United States to maintain civil order. This is a crisis." There was no objection from the members of Congress.

"Ron, I want you to head up the task force to allocate the resources for the electrical crises. I want equal numbers of members from the parties, members of the military and I want several citizens. I want this committee to meet by the day after tomorrow and begin allocating resources. I will not tolerate delay. I will decide disagreements that are not resolved by the committee. Twenty-four hours after meeting, you will issue your first directives."

"General Edwards, you will place your troops under the direction of Dr. Albertson to enforce the quarantines, and under local law enforcement to maintain civil order. Further, I want all bases locked down and off-base personnel moved onto base."

He turned toward the monitor. "Doctor, you have unlimited authority to order the manufacture of smallpox vaccine. That includes appropriating any facilities you deem necessary. Our first priorities for distribution of vaccine stocks are medical personnel, law enforcement and our troops."

He turned toward FBI Director Athena Brown and then toward Albert Bowers, Director of Homeland Security. He was always struck by how similar Bowers looked to actor George Kennedy. "You will pursue these suspects with all diligence. I want to know who they are and who is behind this bio-attack. Do whatever you need to get them. You will work together. This is a joint effort." They both nodded.

"Lastly, George," he pinned the tall slender NSA Director, George Pickering, with a stare, "you and CIA Director, Dave Kennedy will go after those behind this cyber attack." Pickering's shaved head nodded, his gray eyes fixed on the president. Kennedy ran a hand through his graying hair, obviously knowing a large task lay ahead.

He looked at each person attending, including Dr. Albertson. "Text me questions and concerns. We will meet here tomorrow evening. I expect results. I will not tolerate excuses." President Jack Donaldson watched everyone file out. He was scared.

Chapter Thirteen

September 13
Casa Grande, Arizona

It seemed eerie to look out over the unlit gloom of the valley below. A few of the houses had lights, but most were dark. How easily and quickly we revert to primitives, dependent on the sun, thought Kiki. A hundred years of progress gone in a day. Maybe it wasn't a measure of progress. She turned as Nick approached.

"I talked to Brad again. This is an attack, and it's serious. The president has deployed U. S. troops to the large cities. The National Guard will be here tomorrow. They're bringing fresh water and food."

"Troops! Why are they being deployed?" Kiki's mind raced. This would only happen in cases of dire national emergency.

"It's more than a cyber attack. There's been a bio-attack, too. The troops are to enforce a quarantine."

"Bio-attack," gasped Kiki. "What kind of agent? What is the disease?"

"Smallpox."

"But there are vaccines for that. Smallpox was one of the vaccines we received before we went to Afghanistan."

"It's true. We did get smallpox, along with many others, mostly military as part of a broad spectrum vaccine. But most of the people in the world have not been vaccinated. That program stopped in the '70s. The government is trying to crank up the production as quickly as possible, but it will be months before any quantities are available. This could get really ugly."

"Nick, will your family be all right here?" How bad could it get, she wondered. How long could it last?

"Actually, Brad asked if his family could stay with us. Mom agreed. He's going to bring them up during his break. We're pretty safe here, unless everything really goes to hell. Dad never planned on Armageddon, but not only are we self-sufficient, we have a first rate security system. We can defend ourselves if necessary."

Kiki's mind rebelled at the thought of using weapons against fellow citizens. If the sheriff wanted his family out of town, this didn't look good. She felt Nick's arm around her. Together, the two of them could face anything. At least she wanted to believe that.

Troops! Her military mind kicked in. The United States was under attack! Yet there were no foreign forces on U. S. soil, at least not in the conventional sense. Bombs were not being dropped, the military was not being attacked.

Wars were always about resources. Those who could bring the strongest resources to bear would win. Our resources are not even focused on an enemy. This was a battle without bullets. This was a new kind of warfare. The prize was not the United States. The prize was domination of the world economy, and the U. S. economy was headed for the toilet. This was not a war, it was destruction.

She wanted to fight, but how could she fight an enemy that wasn't there? What was the target? The U. S. military would be fighting its own people.

"Nick, there has to be an offensive plan. Whoever initiated this must be attacked."

"Brad mentioned that law enforcement has received photos of suspects. The instructions are to not approach. Maintain surveillance. They must not be killed. This bulletin went out nationwide." Obviously, they wanted prisoners to question, Nick thought. They had to find out more. Somebody had declared war on the United States.

Chapter Fourteen

September 14
Washington, D.C.

FBI Director Athena Brown smiled at the faces around the table. "Mr. President, we got our first break. Anatoly Tsaryov was picked up an hour ago. He was in a cab near the Russian Embassy. Before he could say anything, we tased him and hauled him off. He's at our headquarters in LA. So far, all he's said is he wants diplomatic immunity. We're ignoring that request. We also found Yegor Nikulin, the man in Seattle. As we closed in, he killed himself."

"That is indeed good news. We need information from Tsaryov fast." The president looked at Albert Bowers, Homeland Security Director, and David Kennedy, CIA Director. "Any ideas on how to do that?" He stood, motioning the others to remain seated. He paced a few steps.

Not legally, thought David Kennedy, shaking his head. "Russian agents are hardened against interrogation. Our successes with them involve months of breaking them down, then offering them a carrot. That would mean asylum. Are we really going to offer him that?" His eyebrows rose. He needed to know how far he could go, that he had support to use whatever methods would work. Times like these turned his hair gray.

The president stopped pacing, his face growing red. "We don't have months."

"Mr. President," Bowers said, "two years ago, before your election, we had terrorists in this country murdering the dependents of personnel serving overseas. Perhaps you remember."

"I remember something about it. You solved those cases and stopped them."

"Yes, sir, together with the CIA and the FBI, we did. What's important here is the way we stopped them. We hired two contractors to help capture and interrogate suspects. They accomplished in hours what would take us weeks." Bowers didn't want to say that their methods weren't legal. That would be too much information for the president. He was better off remaining ignorant. In this emergency, legal was a luxury they couldn't afford.

"Can we get them back?" asked the president, leaning on the table.

"Unfortunately, they were killed in a helicopter crash," said David Kennedy. "Dianne Coleman was behind in filing reports. The information is somewhat sketchy. However, the CIA had another contractor training with them. She might be able to help."

"What about the agents you had working with them?" asked the president, glancing at Kennedy, then Bowers.

Kennedy spoke, "Dianne Coleman, the CIA Special Agent, suffered a mental breakdown. I'm afraid she cannot help us."

The president looked at Athena Brown. "Do you know who the FBI agent was?"

The FBI Director tapped on her tablet. "Sir, Special Agent Freddy Foster is presently assigned to the Butte, Montana office. I can bring her in today."

"Do it. Dave, find that contractor who was working with them. Bring her in."

"Sir, she was with Mossad. A word from you would help."

"I'll call as soon as we're finished. Athena, keep on the trail of the other terrorists." The president looked at the monitor. "Doctor Albertson, where are we on the vaccine program?"

"Mr. President, I notified several drug manufacturers that they will dedicate lines to vaccine production immediately. At first, there was objection, but I used your name as a club, threatening to bring in troops to supervise. A call from you would help."

"I'll do it. Give me the contact information. Keep me apprised of the schedule. What about the quarantines?"

"Sir, we have identified the sites for quarantines and given them to General Edwards. I have named group leaders for each site to direct treatment efforts, coordinate with the hospitals and assign medical personnel."

"Not much sleep, huh, Joel?"

"To paraphrase, 'Time enough to sleep when we're dead.'"

"Well put. General Edwards, how are the deployments coming?"

"Sir, I have deployed battalions to each of the sites identified by Doctor Albertson. Troops began moving in last night. Logistical support has arrived and is setting up headquarters at each site. The commander at each site is coordinating with the National Guard commander. Sir, we need to declare Marshall Law. I'd also like to raise our defense status to DEFCON 3. With our focus inside the country, I don't want to let our guard down to threats from outside."

"Good work." He looked at his NSA Director. The man's shaved head gleamed. Did he polish it? "George, how's NSA coming with tracing the source of the cyber attack?"

"Mr. President, our suspicion is that it originated in North Korea. We're trying to refine that trace now. We have been able to limit further hacks."

"Good." The president turned toward Carson. "Ron, what's happening with the electric grid?"

"We've used up the warehouse stock of transformers and control equipment and managed to get several cities back on line." On another monitor, a map of the country showed large red areas over Los Angles, San Francisco, Seattle, Denver, Phoenix, Dallas, Houston, Chicago, New Orleans, Atlanta, Miami, Washington D.C. Philadelphia, and New York.

"We have been able to restore power to more than half, but they are operating with rolling brownouts."

Many of the cities on the monitor turned from red to pink.

"Accomplishing this has depleted our spare parts. We are seeking parts from Canada, Mexico and Europe. China has agreed to move us up on the priority manufacture list, though the price went up 400 percent."

"Bastards," muttered the president.

"The governors have deployed National Guard troops to the larger cities to help with the distribution of food, water and medical supplies. Their presence will also reduce the risk of riots. Smaller cities and towns have put law enforcement on overtime to patrol. It's only been three days. Civil unrest will rear its ugly head in the near future." Ron was clearly worried about the civil situation.

"Those communities without power face multiple risks. The elderly and infirm will be helpless. Food supplies are dwindling. As conditions deteriorate, there will be riots and looting. Fire is a major danger. Without water, firefighters cannot put out fires. There is a real possibility of major fires, so law enforcement personnel will be very aggressive toward rioters.

I agree with General Edwards," Ron nodded at the general, "we need Marshall Law nationally. Governors are already locking down the cities. We will need to get them help as overtime can only go so far. This will be long-term."

Visions whole sections of cities afire rose in many of those around the table. "As much as I hate to do it, with the deployment of troops and the quarantines, you are right," said the president.

Looking at Jackman, his Chief of Staff, he said, "Draft a declaration for me. I'll announce it tonight. We need to get communications back to the nation. Ron, work on that in your spare time. General Edwards, I want the military presence to be highly visible. Troops on the corners, birds in the air, armor on the ground, whatever you think will make people think twice about rioting. Gentlemen and ladies, this is an ugly picture of America."

Chapter Fifteen

September 15
Washington, D.C.

Freddy Foster found herself alone on a small FBI jet winging toward Washington D.C. with no understanding of what happened. "Just following orders," was the only comment. Were they finally going to prosecute her for the gigantic screw up with Dianne Coleman, Nick Sabino and Katherine Russell? After two years, she decided Nick and Katherine were dead, killed in the helicopter crash, even though no traces had been found. The fear of being hunted by them subsided, the whisperings in her mind eased. Peace had come to her in Butte.

Once she understood her rise within the FBI was over, she started to enjoy life again, a life much different from the rat-race pace in Washington D.C. Were they putting her back into what she hoped was behind her? She clamped down on fear before it rose, something she'd learned to do over the last two years.

Could this have something to do with the declaration of Marshall Law her office received yesterday? Butte had power. They hadn't been hit by the outages seen in the rest of the country. They had also received an alert about the outbreak of smallpox in Seattle. The hospitals were on notice, but no cases had appeared. She could not picture Marshall Law in the large cities. What a nightmare that would be. Surely, the FBI had more important things to attend to than her case, didn't they? She relaxed. They probably needed agents in Nome or something. Freddy laughed to herself. Once upon a time that would have been important.

The clunk of the landing gear startled her. She must have dozed. At the small hangar she remembered from her time in D.C. the stairway eased down. Awaiting her was FBI Director Athena Brown. A man in a gray suit held the door of the black Ford open for them.

"I'm Athena Brown."

Freddy looked at the offered hand, then shook it.

"Freddy Foster. Why am I here?"

Athena smiled at the abrupt question. "Almost three years ago you worked a case with Dianne Coleman to thwart a terrorist organization in the U. S."

Freddy's heart thumped. "Yes, I remember it well."

"Let's back up a few steps. The United States is under attack. Have you heard about it?"

"We got the memo, but no details," said Freddy.

"It's a two pronged attack, one a cyber attack that shut down the power grid in much of the nation. The other is a bio-attack with the smallpox virus."

Freddy's mind leapt into gear. She hadn't felt this sensation since the terrorist case. "How can I help?"

"Your team used interrogation techniques that were accurate and fast. We've captured one of those responsible for the smallpox attack. We need to know what he knows."

Freddy stuttered, "I – I never participated in those interrogations. I only observed. We used contractors because the methods were... unusual. And illegal," she admitted.

The car pulled into the garage under the FBI building. As they got out, she recognized Albert Bowers waiting for them.

"Freddy, good to see you again." They shook hands. "Has Athena explained things to you?"

Freddy nodded.

The conference room was one of the smaller ones. Three people stood as she entered. "Freddy, this is Ron Carson, Secretary of the Interior." A handsome dark-haired man rose. She shook his hand. "The uniformed gent is General Tom Edwards, Secretary of Defense." She shook his hand, feeling awed by the company. Another man, gray-haired and slightly pudgy, rose, offering his hand. "This is David Kennedy, Director of the CIA."

His dark eyes stared at her. "Please sit. We need to know everything you know about the interrogations carried out in your case. The country is in a state of crisis. Rules went out the window. It's results we must have."

If this was meant to calm her concerns, it almost worked. Start at the beginning, she thought. "Three years ago, the family of Katherine Russell was slaughtered – murdered and beheaded. That family included her mother, father, husband and six-year-old daughter." The horror she felt dredging up this memory was not reflected in the faces around the table.

"Katherine was one of the most successful snipers in modern warfare, with the highest number of kills in Afghanistan. After the failed attempt to ambush her, a team was sent to America to kill her family. The ploy worked. She returned to the United States for the services. Rather than go back to the Army, she began to hunt down the killers." Freddy paused. Some of those at the table knew this. It was obviously news to others.

"With a partner, Nick Sabino, a medic who saved her life, they pursued the killers. The terror program had expanded beyond Katherine to other service dependents. Local law enforcement for Tucson began an investigation that expanded to Albuquerque, where another slaughter happened. When they realized this might be an international terrorist program, I was called in. I brought in Homeland Security and the CIA." Albert Bowers nodded as he recalled events. David Kennedy was all ears. Much of this was not in the files. It was news to him. Athena Brown was not involved at the time. It was all new to her. She was trying to understand.

"They used an isolation chamber in the questioning. Nick was a genius at manipulating the subjects to tell everything. All this was done without any physical damage.

"Can you describe this isolation chamber?" asked Athena. "I'm not familiar with it."

"It was a box, like an enlarged casket into which the victims, er, subjects were placed. It's a sensory deprivation chamber. Those inside have no contact with the outside world, no sensory input to the brain. They can't see, hear or feel anything physical. Nick Sabino used skillful questioning and a cocktail of drugs to convince the subjects they were dead." Freddy looked at a strange array of expressions on the faces of those around the table.

"Their information proved accurate every time. They killed the first members of the murder team after they were questioned. All this was done on their own. In a botched attempt to seize the leader, Katherine was captured. Nick turned to the authorities for help in getting her back. We did rescue her, but the leader, Hashim al Zaqiri escaped. We held Katherine in custody and persuaded Nick to contract with us for her return." Freddy saw no reaction to this blackmail of citizens in the faces of those at the table.

"We managed to capture al Zaqiri. That was the first interrogation we observed through a streaming link. Nick also returned another member of the terrorist team to us for further questioning. We got nothing from him. He was hopelessly insane." Freddy was looking for any expression of sympathy from those at the table. There was none.

"Al Zaqiri was the last member of the terrorist team on U. S. soil. This team did not do the actual killing. They employed Outlaw Motorcycle Gangs and paid them with raw heroin. We picked up the leader of a Salt Lake City chapter and turned him over to Nick and Katherine. He gave up priceless information about OMGs in the United States. We also learned that the international connection came through drug cartels in Mexico." Freddy looked at the faces around the table. They were focused on every word.

"At this point, we moved Nick and Katherine's operation off-shore onto a boat we'd taken in a drug operation. Nick and Katherine did not want to participate in drug policing and wanted out. Dianne Coleman refused. She wanted to use them in other operations. Dianne brought in a Mossad agent to observe and keep them in line. She threatened them with prosecution and imprisonment. Dianne flew out to the boat to oversee an interrogation of a drug cartel leader, instructing the captain of the boat to head for Guantanamo."

Freddy hated this part. She should have objected. She should have stopped the operation. She hadn't. "Could I have some water?"

Bowers handed her a bottle. She swallowed half the bottle and gathered herself for the rest of the story. "Our audio/video link went down, so I didn't' know what was going on. Somehow, Katherine and Nick overpowered Dianne. They removed Julio Cardenas from the chamber and placed Dianne inside. With the unconscious Cardenas wrapped in a blanket, they hijacked the helicopter. The pilots were forced away by Katherine with a pistol. They assumed it was Dianne in the blanket." Freddy swallowed. She'd avoided this memory for a long time. She took a breath.

"The helicopter disappeared. We never found it or any remains. After three weeks, we abandoned the search. Most of the people who went into the chamber were awake for only hours during the actual questioning. After three days, someone thought to look in the chamber. Dianne's breakdown seems complete. I understand she has moments of clarity, but they are infrequent and short."

"That's quite a story. Let's take a break," said Albert Bowers, rising. Perhaps you'd like to freshen up a bit," he looked at Freddy.

She nodded. Dredging this up had been difficult. Where was this going? A nasty suspicion arose. Would she have to relive it, do this again?

Chapter Sixteen

September 15
Casa Grande, Arizona

Brad finally got a break and a chance to visit his family. As sheriff, he'd gotten no time off, no sleep. He was beat. Before going to the Sabino home, he'd stopped by his house. Though it looked fine, he was glad the family was not there. Jenna and the boys greeted him at the Sabino house door. After the hugs and kisses, they went out on the patio. It was warm as the sun sank behind the horizon.

"Want to take a dip or maybe a Jacuzzi?" asked Nick. "We have extra suits if you forgot yours. Stephen's fixing a gourmet dinner. We've been eating well with him here. Maybe too well." Nick patted his stomach. "Want a drink? Scotch, as I remember."

"If I have a drink, I'll pass out. Maybe after dinner." Brad turned to Miriam Sabino. "I can't thank you enough for putting up with us. My family is one worry I don't have with them here."

"Brad, we're more than happy to have them visit for a while. You do look exhausted. Has it been rough?" asked Miriam.

"The arrival of the Guard really helped. We've been pulling triple shifts and then some. As chief, I couldn't leave until things were organized. We've set up food and water distribution points at the schools throughout the city. So far, people are taking it pretty well." He sighed.

"The president's announcement that we've been attacked by a foreign power went a long way. Most got the message through emergency radios or by word of mouth. People are pulling together. Without that announcement, we'd have demonstrations and riots. Some places have small generators, so people are still buying gas and groceries, but it's on a cash-only basis.

"Another thing that really helped was being able to put some of the agricultural water pumps on the city system. Farmers gave them up, knowing they'd lose this year's crop. I think we'll be able to get some electricity from the power plant in Gila Bend." The corners of Brad's mouth turned up, almost a smile. They were lucky, he thought.

"The distribution system to California is still down. Palo Verde Nuclear is getting some power into Phoenix, though it's rolling blackouts. People get power for four hours twice a day. That's enough to keep refrigerators running. Water is the biggest problem there. There have been riots, and parts of the city burned. No water to fight the fires. So far, they're keeping a lid on it. The Army is holding people in the city or we'd be flooded with refugees." He looked out at the valley, quiet for a moment.

"What about Tucson? Any word on what's happening there?" asked Kiki.

"It's in better shape than Phoenix. Tucson uses a lot of gas driven pumps, so they've kept water flowing, though conservation is a must. Tucson has local auxiliary generating plants that allow some power, though not enough for the whole city. They also get power from the Sulfur Springs Cooperative. That helps. It wasn't hit in the attack."

"Brad, is there anything we can do?" asked Nick. "We're just sitting up here. Both Kiki and

I have training." Nick clasped her hand. She smiled at him.

"Thanks, Nick, Kiki. At this point, we're not organized enough to know how to use help. Considering our country has been attacked, Casa Grande's really not in bad shape. Reports from Los Angeles are bad. The Army put a division around it. Nobody in or out. Sections of the city are quarantined with fences and guards. That's scary." He shook his head. "Demonstrations and riots are met with deadly force. Hundreds have been shot, others sent to detention camps. The Rose Bowl is one of the largest. There is no tolerance for dissension. I know that sounds bad, but they are sitting on a tinderbox."

"Anybody hungry?" asked Stephen, coming from the kitchen. "Dinner's on."

Barb and Stephen had set a beautiful table. With the table extensions, everybody sat together. They had green chili chilaquiles, refried beans, tostadas, and flan for dessert.

"Wow, what a spread," exclaimed Brad. "I didn't even know I was hungry until now." There was little conversation, as mouths were full.

"I'm stuffed." Brad pushed back. "Couldn't eat another bite." He yawned.

"Brad, why don't you and Jenna go on to bed," said Kiki, with a smile. "Nick and I can clean up the dishes and watch the kids. They'll be playing video games anyway. Miriam, I think you, Stephen and Barb could use some fresh air after making that meal. We'll join you on the patio when we're done."

She watched Stephen grab a bottle of Chianti and three glasses as they headed out. Jenna propped up Brad as they went downstairs to their bedroom. I hope he's not too tired, thought Kiki.

The valley below had small islands of light. Only a few headlights moved along the streets. People were staying in their homes. To the east, little traffic flowed on I-10. Below them, I-8 was empty.

Chapter Seventeen

September 15
Casa Grande, Arizona

Kiki started toward the bathroom. Their lovemaking had seemed desperate to her. She turned to the bed. "Nick, this is wonderful here, but if things get bad in the city below, they'll see our lights. At some point someone will want to check us out, maybe more." She watched a look of concern cross Nick's face.

"I know. If the cordon around Los Angles breaks, or people in San Diego get out, there will be a flood of refugees with nothing to lose. I want to show you something." He took her hand and led her to the mirror wall at the back of the bedroom. He pushed a panel and the glass opened. Guiding her, they moved behind the mirror to a stairway.

"Where does this go?" she asked.

"Got your hiking boots on?" Nick smiled.

The circular stairway seemed endless. Kiki guessed they had gone down at least two-hundred feet before they came to a concrete floor. Nick flipped on the lights. Before them was an SUV, suspended on blocks, the tires off the ground. The hood was open and a battery charger was connected. She looked a question at Nick.

"Dad wanted another way out. This passageway leads to a door on the other side of the mountain. In an emergency, we can escape through here." He gazed down the tunnel. Turning to her, he said, "I hope we never have to use it. It means we have abandoned our home."

The climb back up was long. Kiki's mind was trying to picture Nick's dad. What kind of man was he to have foreseen eventualities like this? She wished she'd known him.

Kiki and Nick lay in each other's arms, the soft darkness like a warm blanket. For a few minutes, the troubled world was remote. Like a sparkler going off in their heads, they shivered.

"Oh no, Nick. Not the Director," wailed Kiki.

"I hoped we were rid of it," said Nick.

"Hello Katherine. Hello Nick."

The voice echoed in their heads. A jolt went through both of them. The entity, the Director was back! Kiki pulled Nick close as if he could be a shield.

"Nick. I hoped this beast had left us when we sailed away from Cayman," Kiki cried. She immediately clamped down on her fear and hatred of this being, this thing that fed on human emotion. They both had learned to do that when it haunted them two years ago. This Director was able to implant suggestions to direct human actions and elicit emotions like fear and hatred, the ones it liked to devour the most. And now, it was back.

"Why are you here?" asked Kiki, shuddering. She felt Nick pull her tight.

"It has been so long since we have talked. Are you happy to hear my voice?"

"We haven't missed you, if that's what you're asking," said Kiki.

"I am hurt. And after I helped you."

"You did," said Nick. "You probably saved our lives, but the idea of feeding our emotions to you, or through our actions creating fear or hatred for you to eat is very disgusting to us. Those emotions involve pain and harm to people."

What do you want?" snapped Kiki. "Have your appetites changed?"

"Ho ho! Not at all. The emotions of hatred and fear are still my favorite meals. No, I am here to tell you that I have been observing the attack on your country. Feasting in Los Angeles has been good. But that is not all I have to tell you. The FBI is asking Freddy Foster to help them catch those responsible. After you disappeared, she was held responsible for the mess. What you did to Dianne Coleman has given me many nice meals when she is lucid enough to be frightened. Freddy was banished to Butte, Montana. Now she is back in Washington. All is forgiven with her. Perhaps you should contact her. I would suggest it. Ta ta".

"God, Nick. Life was so good without that Director. None of the other entities tried to contact us. I wouldn't have minded the ones that feast on love or caring."

"How do you know?" he asked.

"The idea of a being living off the grief and misery of humans repels me."

What do you think about the message?" he asked. "We'd be exposing ourselves."

"Nick, in the long run, we couldn't live our lives hidden here. And I'm not anxious to go back to the boat. I'm enjoying the feel of earth under my feet."

"I want to stay here with my family. We have to take the risk. We'll send Freddy an email tomorrow."

Kiki nodded in the dark. The vision of them standing on a cliff above a fog-shrouded valley appeared. They were about to step off into what?

Chapter Eighteen

September 16
Washington, D.C.

The break suggested by Albert Bowers had lasted past midnight. Freddy was weary, but the sense of urgency in facing this crisis pushed her on. She offered a smile she didn't feel.

"Freddy, the president is sitting in on this meeting." He motioned toward a monitor.

President Jack Donaldson looked at her. "Agent Foster, it is critical you understand you have my full backing to do anything you can to assist us. I'm going to listen in. Proceed, David."

"Where is the equipment, the isolation chamber Nick and Katherine used?" asked David Kennedy.

"I believe it is still at Guantanamo. The boat was stored there, the contents sequestered. You can check easily enough." Freddy felt the needles of apprehension crawl up her spine at the thought of opening this Pandora's box she'd so carefully locked away.

"Do you think you can operate it?" asked Athena Brown.

Freddy took a breath. "No. I was never physically present during an interrogation. Whatever Nick did with the drugs was hidden from me. The tapes of the questioning should be available." She looked at the FBI Director.

"The boat was sealed. Everything should be on board," Athena said.

"Freddy, what about this other agent used by Dianne Coleman?"

"I only knew her as Zyra. She was part of a Mossad team hired by the Mexican government to fight the cartels. Her assignment from Dianne was to learn how to follow in Nick's footsteps. At some point, Dianne decided to get rid of Nick and Katherine. Other than them, she is the most competent, though Nick had a talent that cannot be taught."

"We will ask Israel for Zyra's services," said the president. "I will call as soon as this meeting is over. We want you to head up a team to interrogate suspects in this attack."

"Freddy, we're going to Guantanamo. You can sleep on the plane. We need to know what equipment to bring back," said Ron Carson. "Mr. President, thank you for your support."

"No, Freddy, Ron, thank you for your service," said the president. The screen went dark.

The same car waited for them in the basement parking. The same plane waited in the hangar.

"Freddy, I know you haven't slept in a while. In the bathroom is everything you need," said Ron, pointing to the rear of the plane. "If it's not there, let me know. There's a change of clothes in the closet at the back, including PJs, if you want them. The back seats fold down to full beds. A curtain will give you some privacy. I might suggest a glass of chardonnay to help you sleep, but it's your call. I have some work to do, so I'll be up. Get some rest. It may the last for a while."

Freddy had never seen a shower in an airplane bathroom before. The chardonnay did help.

The clunk of the landing gear woke her. While she was getting ready for the day, her iPhone toned an email message.

Perhaps we can help. You won't arrest us, will you? N. Sabino, K. Russell

HOLY SHIT!

She rushed forward waving the iPhone. Ron Carson was on the phone. When he saw the look on her face, he begged off the call. She showed him the text.

"It's Nick and Katherine! I thought they were dead." She realized she was shouting. Her mouth snapped shut.

"Text them back. Ask if they would feel comfortable giving you a contact number."

She did. A phone number appeared.

Ron placed a call. "Mr. President, we've had another break. It seems that Nick Sabino and Katherine Russell are alive and offering their services. I'd like to tie you in on a three-way call to them. They need assurance. Coming from you would go a long way. Hold on."

Ron pressed buttons and handed the phone to Freddy. The call was picked up on the first ring.

"Nick, this is Freddy Foster. We need your help."

"Mr. Sabino, this is President Jack Donaldson. I repeat what Ms. Foster said, we need your help. We are in a crisis. I can have a plane pick you up wherever you want in thirty minutes."

"Mr. President, Freddy, okay, I'm a little awed here. Kiki and I want to help. We're in Casa Grande, Arizona. Tell me where you want us to go."

Ron spoke up. "The runway in Casa Grande is too short. We can have you picked up by helicopter, but I think it's almost as fast for you to drive. Can you get to the Air National Guard station at Pinal Airpark?"

"We can be there in forty-five minutes," said Nick.

"Tell the gate guard who you are. We will have planes waiting," said Ron.

"Mr. President, I'll make the arrangements to have a couple of F-16s there. If you could call General Edwards so he can facilitate the flights and arrange for in-flight refuel, we can have them in Guantanamo in less than five hours."

"Nick, Katherine, thank you. I look forward to meeting you," said the president.

"See you a few hours." said Freddy.

Freddy looked at Ron. He was on the phone again. For the first time in years, she felt good, alive again and part of something bigger than herself. She looked down. Still in her PJs. She almost skipped to the back of the plane.

Chapter Nineteen

September 16
Casa Grande, Arizona

"Nick, Kiki, do you believe it was really the president speaking?" asked Brad.

"I do," said Kiki. "I recognized his voice."

"Why would he call personally?" Brad persisted.

"It was a smart move," said Kiki. "By calling himself, he assured us he was aware of our past and sanctioned what is needed to end this crisis. His call also was his way of telling us this is a real crisis, not one manufactured by the press." At least this is what she needed to believe.

"Brad, last night, we talked about staying in this country." Kiki put her hand on Nick's arm. She looked back at Brad. "We cannot do that underground. This is our chance to remain permanently. Besides, we both want to do something to help."

"What are you going to be doing?" Brad's eyebrows rose.

Kiki gave him a hard stare, assessing what to say. "Probably the same type of things we did with the last terrorists." Were they ready to do that again? Destroying men's souls had driven her away before. This was different, she told herself. But was it?

Kiki and Nick put their smallish kits in the SUV. Kiki smiled at the sun rising in the clear blue sky. Everything would be provided, they'd been told. As they pulled out of the driveway, Nick and Kiki waved at the family. The Pinal Air Park was down Interstate 10, an easy drive. Would they see them again, Kiki wondered. So much could happen.

The gate guard approached their car. Nick rolled the window down. "Nick Sabino and Katherine Russell."

"Thank you, sir. Proceed on this road toward that large hangar." The guard pointed. "They are waiting for you."

A soldier waved them into a parking space beside the hangar. "Follow me." They went into the hangar. Two airmen were waiting with flight-suits. The woman took Kiki into a locker room while Nick went into another locker room. The airman pointed at the toilet. Nick used it. After a bit of wrestling themselves into the suits, they emerged. On the other side of the hangar were two F-16s, their engines idling. Aides strapped them in, put helmets on them, patted the pilots on the shoulders and moved away. Nick waved at Kiki in the other plane. She waved back.

In tandem, the planes taxied to the end of the runway. The canopy closed. With a roar, Nick was pushed back into the seat as the plane shot down the runway. Suddenly he was looking at sky. His G-suit inflated, squeezing him, as he felt crushing weight pressing down. Blackness came up, his vision narrowed. He lost track of time. Pressure eased, as the plane leveled out, then it kicked him again as it accelerated. The roar of the engine stopped. They'd gone supersonic.

Time passed. The plane slowed and the roar of the engine shook him again. Ahead was another plane. He was sure they were going to collide. A winged pipe stuck out. They were refueling. Minutes later, they moved aside and Nick watched Kiki's plane gulp fuel from the giant tanker. Both planes rose, and again, the acceleration punched him, the engine noise faded.

The engine noise rocked him as the plane descended. Within minutes, the landing gear clunked down. They hit the ground with a feathery touch. The canopy opened as they taxied. Aides helped him out and into another hangar. His body felt stiff and sore. Kiki joined him.

"Was that a great ride or what!" She beamed at him.

Inside the hangar, Freddy Foster stood, waiting for them. She reached out, shaking Nick's hand first. She turned to Kiki and gave her a hug. "You don't know how glad I am to see you. We have so much to talk about. Go ahead and change clothes. Are you hungry? Can I get you anything?" She shooed them toward the locker room.

This was not the same Freddy Foster they met before, mused Nick. The intensity in her manner from two years ago was muted. She had changed, but what had changed her? The Director said she feared for her life at the hand of him and Kiki. Perhaps looking over her shoulder for two years until her fear burned out had done it. What had she been doing in that two years?

Chapter Twenty

September 16
The Democratic People's Republic of Korea

Lieutenant Gun Rahn was worried. The Americans had blunted the cyber attack, and his continued haranguing of his technicians had not resulted in bypassing the newly constructed firewalls. Failure in North Korea was not accepted well. A bead of sweat rolled down his forehead. He dare not wipe it away while standing at attention before Captain Han-jae.

"Relax, Lieutenant. We knew the Americans would find a way to stop our continued hack on the power grid. Our attack has accomplished its aim. Enough equipment has been damaged that parts of their grid will be down for months, if not a year. It is time to initiate the second phase of our cyber war."

He handed Lieutenant Rahn a sealed envelope. "Study this. Give your technicians only the information they need to hack into the American's internet system. Remember, our intent is to compromise their security, not destroy the internet. We need it intact to continue our war. We want to know what they are doing. That is all."

Lieutenant Rahn saluted smartly. Captain Han-jae returned it with a dismissive wave. Whew, he thought as he returned to the control center. He had not been sure he would survive that meeting. At his desk he opened the envelope. Before him was a list of codes and passwords that would get them into the American's system.

He studied it, deciding who would best accomplish the tasks laid out. With the hack start date tomorrow, he could give his men the night off. They were exhausted. His team had been at it for five days without a break. He looked over the floor of the center from his office window. He went out onto the elevated walkway, glad to be able to give his men some good news.

"Attention," his sergeant cried. The technicians stopped, and stood at attention, facing him.

"Comrades, you have done your duty well these last five days. Tomorrow we begin a new assault on the American systems. Go home to your families tonight. Be ready tomorrow."

Smiles broke out. The men talked among themselves as they filed out the door. "Sergeant, take the day off. You deserve it." Sergeant Ryang snapped him a salute, spun on his heel and headed for the door.

Back at this desk, Gun looked at the file. His mind began to wonder, something he could only do when he was alone. Where had these codes come from? There had to be agents in America who secured them.

A more troubling thought arose. What would the Americans do? The hacks would be traced to them. They had already demonstrated that ability when Gun and his team hacked into commercial business, particularly Sony after they released the propaganda film calling for his commander's death. The DPRK could not tolerate freedom of communication inside the country. The retaliation had damaged their computer systems and the internet, but they had recovered. China, their only ally, had helped them bypass the sanctions imposed.

There would be retaliation, of that he was sure. The economy in the People's Republic was already in shambles. It was only through the iron fist of control that uprisings were averted. An attack on the economy would be ineffectual.

The thing about a cyber war, no troops left the country, no troops invaded the enemy, no bullets were fired. Would the Americans escalate to a physical war or choose to keep this conflict on an electronic level? How could the Americans truly hurt the DPRK? That was the question.

Chapter Twenty-One

September 17
Koltsovo, Russia

Yehvah Balakina hated the middle of the month. It was her time to check the inventory of stored viral agents at the Vector Institute. She had been Security Specialist First Class at the Institute in Koltsovo for only a year, and still took her duties seriously. She squared her shoulders, pushed her sandy hair from her eyes. This was the last refrigerated bunker to check, and the chill of inspecting the previous five had worked its way through her coat.

As she opened the door, the blast of cold air hit her face. Her breath rose in clouds. Stacked on each side of the aisle were plastic containers labeled variola major h. She was not a scientist. The labels meant nothing. At the end of the row was an opened pallet with two twenty-liter jugs missing. She looked at her inventory list. Any removal of materials should have been logged. It did not show that. Perhaps, some scientists had removed the forty liters for testing or study and not amended the inventory list. She noted it.

Exiting the bunker, she went to the guardhouse. "Kirill, why was my inventory list not updated to show the removal of two jugs of," she looked at the list, "variola major h from bunker six?" She straightened her back, trying to make her five foot-four inch frame taller and hopefully more intimidating.

He turned watery eyes on her. "When did this happen?"

Drunk again, she thought. He was worthless as a guard. "I don't know. There is nothing on my list. Let me see the entry log." She plucked the book from the shelf. Few people visited the cold storage bunkers, so the pages for the last month were blank. The previous month, August third, Doctor Malikov had entered.

"Kirill, did Dr. Malikov remove two bottles from bunker six?"

Kirill's rheumy eyes again looked at her. "When?" he grunted.

"August third," answered Yehvah.

"That was over a month ago. I don't remember. Go away."

Yehvah marched out of the guardhouse. If she could get him fired, she would. That was impossible. These people had to understand the necessity to follow procedure. She stepped into Malikov's office. He looked up at the intrusion.

"I'm sorry to disturb you, Dr. Malikov." She looked around his office. Papers lay in piles on every surface, books were opened on his desk, an open box was in one corner labeled My Bubbles in English. "Did you remove two containers of variola major h from bunker six last month?"

His mouth fell open, he paled. "I...I don't remember that," he stammered.

A strange reaction, thought Yehvah. "On August third you entered bunker six. It's on the log. Two containers are missing. Did you remove them?"

"I...I didn't do that."

"Why were you in bunker six?" she demanded. "I'm going to have to report this to Major Pushkin." He appeared to calm at the major's name. That was unexpected, she thought. "Where are those jugs now?"

"I used them for testing. They have been destroyed," he stated, regaining his composure.

She turned and left. Behind her, Malikov reached for the phone.

The log at the high temperature furnace should show these entries. No one was in the furnace vault, but the logbook sat on the table. She went to it and thumbed backwards. There was no listing for a quantity of variola major h being incinerated.

Tentatively, she knocked on Major Pushkin's door. Once she reported this, her duty was over. "Come," called the gruff voice.

Yehvah snapped to attention. "Sir, I have encountered a problem with the inventory."

"Eh?" said the major, looking up from behind his desk. He reminded Yehvah of her grandfather, sparse gray hair, a kindly deeply lined face. "Ah, Yehvah, good to see you. What's this you say, a problem?" He motioned her to a chair. I just got a call from Dr. Malikov, something about some jugs he forgot to log. It's not a big problem. We can forget about it. You know these scientists. They don't understand security procedures. We can take care of this."

"Major, there is no record of those jugs being removed, nor any record of them being destroyed, as Dr. Malikov claims. We need to know where they are. If there is an incident like Vozrozhdeniya Island in 1971, we will have people from the World Health Organization all over us." She started to stand.

Pushkin held up a hand, gesturing for her to sit. "Calm yourself, Yehvah. Write up the report and give it to me personally. I'll take care of it. It's just an oversight, nothing serious."

As she closed the door behind her, Pushkin dialed the phone. "Good day, Colonel Noskov, Major Pushkin here. The viral agents we secured for you have been missed. Dr. Malikov did not understand the need to cover his tracks. One of our security staff noted the missing forty liters. I will alter the logs to show the virus was destroyed. I will take care of her if the need arises."

Pushkin hung up the phone. He liked Yehvah, but she was young and still idealistic. He hoped she would not be a problem.

Chapter Twenty-Two

September 17
Guantanamo, Cuba

Kiki and Nick emerged from the locker rooms in light-weight street clothes suitable for the hot and humid conditions in Cuba. They glanced at each other. Street clothes on this base were like visitor badges. Other than Ron Carson and Freddy Foster, all others were in Marine uniform. Kiki and Nick had volunteered for this duty, but the memories of their past as interrogators raised trepidations. Those were experiences they had hoped never to repeat. Yet, here they were.

The drive from Moffett Field on Sherman Avenue to Boat Shed Road took them directly to the covered boat storage. In less than ten minutes, they were looking at the boat where Kiki and Nick had performed their last interrogation. Kiki looked around. This was a different view of Guantanamo from her first visit. Glimpses of chain-link fences along roadways and a concrete cell without windows were all she'd seen.

As she stepped onto the boat, a tremor ran through her. She had put this part of her life behind her, and good riddance it was.

Now she was back on the sixty-five foot boat. Though it had been sealed, dust magically appeared to cover the inside.

Following Nick, the foursome went directly to the stateroom where the isolation chamber had been. Nick switched on the lights. "We had power hooked up," explained Carson. "Anything you need, let us know. We'll get it. We thought about moving the equipment to the U.S."

"I will need to contact my family at least once a week," said Nick.

"I will arrange for it," responded Ron.

The single porthole was opaque, letting light in but no view. On the teak paneled walls were several medical-style monitors. A softly padded chair with a laptop computer sat near the chamber. Two other chairs flanked it. Kiki and Nick approached the large coffin-like box in the center of the room. There was little dust on it, as if the motes were repelled. Its dark surface absorbed light like a black hole. Kiki and Nick opened the top. It was dry inside. "At least someone thought to drain it," said Kiki.

Nick checked sensors and turned on monitors. He spent twenty minutes inspecting the dosimeters. At last, he turned to Freddy. "I'll give you a list of what we need. The equipment seems to be in good shape, but we need to replace sensors, tubes and hoses. The hospital will have most of the medications, but there will be a few that are special. I need to get water circulating to check out the pumps and the heating units."

"Are you going to have the satellite linkup observing us?" asked Kiki. How many people were aware of what they would be doing, she wondered. What kind of records would they keep?

Freddy looked at Ron. "We'd like to, but this is your show. We were arranging to bring in Zyra until you contacted us. Do you want her?"

"Only if we have to kill somebody," said Kiki. The vision of the intense agent and her black eyes and icy manner sent a shiver down her spine.

"We can be online faster if we work here rather than move the equipment," said Nick. "Bring the subjects here. We will need a native speaker for whatever language the subjects speak."

"Our first subject is Russian," said Ron. "We suspect the others associated with the bio-attack are also. Zyra emigrated to Israel from Russia."

"Okay, bring her in," said Kiki. "The fewer people that know about this the better for us." Ron gave her a strange look. He didn't yet understand, she thought.

Nick and I will have a list for you in thirty minutes," said Kiki. It was a dismissal. Ron and Freddy left.

"Nick, are you ready for this, because I'm not sure I am." Of those who knew of their interrogations, only Freddy understood they would rip the souls from their subjects. Freddy had seen the insanity they caused.

"K, part of my training as a medic included some study of smallpox. I want to show you some things." Nick took out his pad. With a few taps, he held it out to her. "Scroll through until you've seen enough."

It was images of smallpox victims in various stages of the disease. Within seconds, Kiki averted her eyes, handing the pad back to Nick.

"Here's something else that Freddy sent me." It was a video of a man handing small pink bottles to children gathered around him. Behind was the unmistakable Magic Kingdom. "That man is giving those children smallpox in Disneyland. This happened less than a month ago. He will be our first patient."

Kiki felt revulsion building up. Hatred rose like a fever. She had to clamp down on it! A prickly chill touched her mind. Oh no, she thought, not it.

"Aah, Katherine, you are back. I missed you."

She looked at Nick, her mouth wide. He had heard it, too. "Nick, we're going to have to keep a lid on our emotions if we don't want the Director back in our lives," she wailed.

"Now, now. Do not be unhappy. I will not try to direct you. There is enough hatred and fear for me to devour in your country now. My appetite for those emotions has taken me from Africa and the Middle East to other places. Your country is becoming a tasty array as these attacks go on. Freddy Foster was sure you were going to return and kill

her. You gave me a year of feeding on her fear. Alas, she has overcome that."

"We weren't going to go after her," said Kiki to the empty room.

"But she did not know that."

"Now that we're going to help defend our country against this attack, you're going to haunt us again?" Kiki shook her head. She didn't need this.

"I like you. You are so much more interesting to talk to than those others of me. Did the sweet side of me talk to you?"

"None of your other entities harassed us," said Nick.

"They have no balls. Ha ha. That is a joke. None of us have balls."

"Very funny. You're developing a sense of humor now?" sneered Kiki.

"I must have gotten that from you. Ha ha. I must go now. There is a wonderful feast at Los Angeles Memorial Hospital. People are trying to break the quarantine. It is sure to be fun. Ta ta. "

Kiki gave Nick a look of despair. She wanted to turn away and run. She felt Nick's hand on her shoulder.

"K, we have to do this."

Chapter Twenty-Three

September 18
The Situation Room
Washington, D.C.

"Dr. Albertson, what is the status of the bio-attack?" asked President Donaldson. All eyes around the conference table were glued to the monitor.

Dr. Albertson wiped his bald head, looking down at the papers he held. "Mr. President, there is no good news. Our quarantine areas in Los Angeles are holding, as are those in San Diego, though there have been riots and casualties. The same for Seattle. The reports of outbreaks along the east coast are now coming in. General Edwards and I agreed to dispatch troops to enforce quarantines in Washington, New York, Boston, and Philadelphia. We have quarantined parts of Atlanta, Chicago and Miami. Fatality rates are 500 per day and rising."

"Mr. President, I need to activate reservists," boomed General Edwards.

"Do it," responded the president. "What about vaccines?"

"Sir, we contacted the Vector Institute in Koltsovo, Russia. It is the only licensed laboratory for the study of smallpox besides us. They claimed to have no vaccines," said Albertson.

"Mr. President," said Dave Kennedy, "the CIA has some resources at Koltsovo. According one of them, they have been manufacturing smallpox vaccines on a crash basis for two months. Unmarked trucks are picking up the shipments. In addition, our source reported missing containers of smallpox."

The conference room was a tableau in stunned silence. "Are these sanctioned actions?" asked the president.

"We're not sure. One source reported the vaccine production and missing containers, the other did not. That may indicate local malfeasance. How high up the ladder it goes is the real question. To protect our one source, we must be cautious what we ask."

"Let's put a satellite over Koltsovo and follow those vaccine trucks," said the president.

"Already done, sir. According to our source, the next shipment is due for pickup tomorrow," said Kennedy. "We're also putting together a group for a possible hijack of the shipment, depending on the destination and route taken."

"Mr. President, we need that vaccine for our law enforcement and troops," said Dr. Albertson. "Our own manufacture won't be up to capacity for months."

"Mr. Bowers, where is Homeland Security on the infrastructure?"

"Mr. President, we have as many of the electrical control systems back on line as possible until new equipment arrives. We're using rolling blackouts as a way of distributing power where we can. Some areas do not have the redundancy and will operate on emergency generators for hospital and law enforcement only. We are trucking in food and water to distribution centers. We are operating on a temporary basis, but this may not be temporary."

The president looked down, shaking his head. "Never before have we been so overwhelmed in our ability to provide for our citizens. George, what has the NSA been able to do in tracking down the source of this cyber-attack?"

"Mr. President, we're ninety percent certain North Korea is behind this attack. The remaining ten percent is because the sophistication of the attack and bypassing our firewalls is beyond North Korea's abilities. We suspect someone else is colluding with them and helped bypass the sanctions,"

"Let's begin planning a response. We won't act on it until we know more." He looked at Robert Chou and Elizabeth Gutierrez, the two Congressional members attending. They nodded approval.

"Athena, what's the FBI got for us?"

"Mr. President, as you know, we captured one suspect and lost another to suicide. We have leads on three others and hope to take them into custody within the week. We also found one of the shooters destroying the transformers, but he killed himself before we could get to him. He appears to be of Asian lineage."

"Ron, where are we in finding out who's behind the bio-attack?"

From another monitor, Ron Carson spoke, "Mr. President, we will begin interrogating our first suspect in a few hours. I'll keep you informed as the interrogation proceeds."

Nobody at the table asked where or how the interrogation would take place. That was information best left unspoken.

Chapter Twenty-Four

September 18
Guantanamo, Cuba

Bent over the chamber making adjustments, Kiki's and Nick's heads popped up as the door to the stateroom opened soundlessly. The figure in the dimness of the passageway was a shadow – tall, thin, and angular. Zyra stepped into the room. Her stern face a frozen mask as she stared at Nick and Kiki. Kiki felt Zyra's eyes bore into her like laser rays. Zyra looked around the room, her gaze resting on the isolation chamber.

"Hello, Zyra," Nick offered. It was obvious the woman was pissed, probably at them. They had outmaneuvered her and escaped. She wasn't someone who tolerated failure, especially in herself.

"We work together again," she stated simply. "This time I am not to watch over you. I am mad at myself for losing you before, but I understand you did what was necessary to survive." She looked at Nick. "I will be interested to watch how you break down a Russian."

Yeah? Nick wondered. How would he break down a Russian? "Do you know any of his background?"

"I tell you first of KGB man background," Zyra responded. "Mostly officers are recruited from military, but others are recruited from gangs. This man we have file on. He is from gang. Criminal background in smuggling, extortion, enforcement, murder for hire. He is low level."

Nick asked, "Anything of a personal background?"

Zyra nodded, frowning. "Father smuggler, mother prostitute. Raised in Catholic Church orphanage until ten. Ran away, lived on street. He is nothing."

What a summary of someone's life, thought Nick. The boat rocked slightly as several people stepped on at the same time. "Our guest has arrived," said Nick.

Ron came in, followed by Freddy and two men with a stretcher. Strapped to it was an unconscious man. Zyra's gaze was fixed on the stretcher.

"Strip him, lay him on the floor," said Nick. "What will be his last memory?" The men looked at him with puzzled expressions. "How was he taken?"

"He was in a cab. We tased him and yanked him out. We gave him an anesthetic. He's been unconscious since." One of the men pulled out a slip of paper and read off the anesthetic used and the amount.

"Photographs front and back," said Nick. The many tattoos would give them valuable information. He looked at Zyra. She nodded understanding.

"Put him in the chamber. Use the soft restraints." Nick watched the monitor on the wall. His weight was 109 kilos. Nick turned to the others. "Kiki, Zyra, please be seated. Ron, Freddy you may stay or leave, your choice." To the two men he said, "Thanks, we'll call you when we need you." The door closed softly behind them.

Looking at Ron and Freddy, he continued, "If you are going to stay, it is important you remain quiet. You can get more chairs from the next stateroom. This session may take hours." He could tell that curiosity was holding them both. Freddy had only seen sessions through a remote link. Ron knew nothing.

Standing over the chamber, Nick looked down as it filled with brine. The man was fit, hard with little fat. His face was older than his body. The tattoos were the backdrop to the scars. Zyra's abbreviated biography was accurate, tough life. Nick made some adjustments until the body floated just right. He inserted several IVs, attached sensor pads, and a bone microphone. With a last look, Nick closed the lid. Goodbye, whoever you were, he thought.

Once in his chair, he used the laptop to set up the medications. He added curanine to paralyze Tsaryov, but not suffocate him. Adrenaline was slowly added, Nick focused on the heart rate, respiration and brain activity traces. "He's waking up. Let's see what he does."

The speaker from the chamber gave out a groan.

Nick explained to Ron and Freddy, "The sound deadening equipment keeps his ears from hearing anything, even himself." There was a yell in Russian.

"He's asking where he is," translated Zyra.

"Say nothing," instructed Nick. He watched heart rate, breathing and brainwave activity pick up. More yelling. Nick watched him struggle to move. He upped the curanine slightly. The yelling increased. Nick let it go on for thirty minutes.

"Tell him to shut up," said Nick, "nothing else."

Zyra complied. The yelling stopped. "He's asking who you are," said Zyra.

Say exactly what I tell you, nothing else, said Nick.

"I am you," said Nick.

Zyra paused then translated. "He is asking how that is possible." She looked at Nick.

"Would you rather I said I was God?" Nick's said.

Zyra stared at him, eyebrows raised. Nick nodded. He glanced at Ron and Freddy. Their faces held puzzled looks. Zyra translated.

"You cannot be God. I learned of God in the orphanage. There is no God. I prayed, I confessed, I begged but God never answer me." The cry from the speakers echoed in the small stateroom.

"No answer is an answer. You asked for things. I do not give things," said Nick.

"What do you give," demanded Tsaryov, his voice rising.

"I will give you what you didn't ask for. I will give you peace, but you must confess your life to me. By telling me, you release those acts to me. I will wash them away. What you do not tell me will sink you into torment forever. Your soul is in the balance."

"You want me to confess, like at the orphanage?" whined Tsaryov.

"Your confessions at the orphanage were hollow, for you never intended to forsake those actions and trust in me."

"Where do I start?" came the plea.

"Start with your last memories."

"I was riding to get to the Russian embassy. I was to start a new mission. These men shoot me. I am frozen, cannot move. I remember nothing after that. They did not torture me or ask me questions. Did they kill me?"

"They took you from your world. What was your mission?"

Tsaryov groaned. "I give these toys to the children that make bubbles. I did that. I visit Disneyland. It was a dream of mine when I was a child. I make them happy."

"You didn't know that there was poison in those bottles?"

"Poison! It was soapy water that makes bubbles. It was not poison. I would not kill children, only make them sick. Others sure, I kill okay if I am told to do it."

"You cannot lie to me! All the children you gave those to are dead. Who sent you on this mission?"

"It was my commandant. Three of us were to do this. From the city Los Angeles, I go to San Diego. Another box of toys was at my hotel. I give those to the children at the place called LEGOLAND. I liked it as much as Disneyland."

"Who is your commandant who told you to do these things?"

"Major Verenich leads our group. He was the commandant when we were the KGB. Now we are another group without a name. These children were not my sin. I didn't know," his voice rising.

"Stop lying. It is another sin. Tell me more of what you did for this group."

Nick watched Ron and Freddy leave. They needed to start tracking down this Major Verenich and the gang he led. The interrogation continued for hours, everything recorded. There would be a lot to pick through and analyze.

Chapter Twenty-Five

September 18
Guantanamo, Cuba

From the helm of the boat, Ron Carson placed a FaceTime call to David Kennedy. The lines on Kennedy's round face seemed deeper. "David, we have something on the bio-attack. Our suspect confessed. We've got a name for the CIA to start on. Major Verenich leads some gang, ex-KGB. It sounds like they are freelance contractors now."

"Good work, Ron. How did you break him down so quickly?"

"I'll tell you about it when we get together. This guy says he didn't know what he was doing. He was just a foot-soldier following orders. He thought he was giving the kids treats that would only make them sick."

"Everybody says that under interrogation," responded Kennedy.

"We will have more for you on this gang later," said Ron, "but I wanted you to get started ASAP so you can start running down info on Verenich."

"I'll be back to you when we have something." David ended the call.

Ron turned to Freddy. "That's a unique interrogation method. I've never seen anything like it."

Freddy frowned. "You should know that all the subjects they interrogated two years ago came out of that chamber insane, like Dianne Coleman. It is more savage in many ways than physical torture."

"I don't understand," said Ron, puzzled. How could this be so bad? He wondered.

A sad look passed over Freddy's face. "The subjects believe they are dead and in the afterlife, with God in this case. The shock of learning they must face death again after confessing everything is too much." She took a deep breath. "The complete isolation and loss of contact with the physical world creates the depth of their belief they are dead. Our brains are not fashioned to be independent from this bodily existence."

"What happened to the other subjects?" Ron asked.

"Their victims were killed before the FBI and the CIA contracted with Nick and Kiki. Those interrogated afterward we worked with them are still alive in an asylum, if you could call their condition alive. That's where Dianne Coleman is, too."

"Tell me what happened with Dianne Coleman. I looked her up. She was a good agent, on the fast-track." Had Sabino and Russell driven her insane? he wondered.

Freddy stared at him before speaking. "She was goal driven, cutting corners and using people. Our deal with Nick and Kiki was to stop the terrorists in the U. S. Once that was done, they were to be free, pardoned for past sins. Dianne was going to force them to go back to Afghanistan by blackmailing them. Later I found out our whole operation was completely unsanctioned."

Ron was surprised. None of this was in the records. Dianne Coleman's disability was listed as a nervous breakdown.

"Nick and Kiki found out and escaped, locking Dianne in the chamber."

Ron shook his head. "Did you try to duplicate the techniques Nick and Katherine use?"

"I was pulled off and given opportunities in remote locations. Someone had to be blamed. The loss of Dianne, Nick and Katherine, the drug lord, and the helicopter rested on my shoulders. I understood Nick and Katherine were in for the terrorist program only, but the intel we were getting on Outlaw Motorcycle Gangs and drug lords was too good. I couldn't let go. I should have called a halt when Dianne went off the rails. I didn't." Freddy looked down, her shoulders slumped.

"That's some deep introspection," noted Ron.

"Remote locations give one that opportunity. Bitterness only turns the assignment into a prison sentence."

"What about Zyra?" asked Ron. "She's...."

"She was originally part of an Israeli team hired by the Mexican government and resort industry to clean up the cartels. Dianne contracted her to learn how to do the interrogations. I heard she was not successful to the same extent." Freddy took a deep breath. "Nick has a talent for figuring how to best get into the head of the subjects. He plays with the right combination of drugs and questions like a virtuoso. You saw how fast he was into Tsaryov's head. There is not a doubt in my mind he can break down anyone. I lived in terror for two years, afraid Nick and Katherine would come after me. I had dreams of a monster eating away at me. Only after I came to grips with myself did those nightmares fade."

Ron's phone rang. He answered.

"David Kennedy here. We have Major Verenich in our system. You were right. He was KGB. When the old USSR broke up, like many others, he formed a gang from his old unit. They are into everything nefarious. The question we have to ask him is who contracted him for this job."

"Ask him? How are we going to do that?"

"Get out your traveling shoes. We're putting together a team now."

Chapter Twenty-Six

September 19

Kiki and Nick sat in the small conference room, the speakerphone on the table. This was his first call home since he and Kiki left. After arriving at Guantanamo, they'd received very little news of happenings on the outside, and nothing from Casa Grande.

"Mom, are things going okay there?"

"It's good to hear your voice, Nick. How are you and Kiki doing?"

"We're fine, Mom. Is everything alright?"

"Well, we've watched news. California looks bad. As Sheriff, Brad is working long hours. He's here now, if you want to talk to him."

His mother was shuffling him off quickly. What was going on? "Mom, are you and Stephen and the kids okay?"

"It's been stressful. It would be better if Brad explained."

"Nick, are you there?" Brad's voice sounded as if he were exhausted.

"Hey, Brad. Are you okay?"

"Yeah, just long hours. Let me go outside."

Nick heard shuffling.

"Hey, I'm back. It's deteriorating here, Nick. The brownouts are putting people on edge. We can control that. Apparently, the smallpox epidemic in California is getting bad. I've received estimates of 500 fatalities a day in Los Angeles. San Diego can't be far behind. Demonstrations are met with force. Troops have fired on advancing crowds with heavy casualties. The quarantine isn't holding. There's now a roadblock and gate at Gila Bend. Anyone coming east on I-8 is put into the old stock pens as a holding facility, and it's filling fast.

"I've vaccinated my guys, but if smallpox hits here, we'll lose control. There's no vaccine for the public."

Nick looked at Kiki. This was bad. "Brad, I can't tell you exactly what we're doing, but we are working on the same problem. I think I can arrange for vaccine for all of you at the house." He wished he could tell him what was going on.

"That would be a relief, Nick. If things go south, this house is pretty strong."

"Brad, have Stephen show you the emergency exit. I'm not saying you'll need it, but the house is not mob proof."

"Thanks, I knew your dad wouldn't get painted into a corner." Nick heard relief in Brad's voice. "Looks like his precautions were not wasted."

Kiki leaned forward toward the speakerphone. "Brad, this is Kiki. If things start to fall apart, go to my mom and... to my ranch. You can find it in the records. The place is remote, has its own windmill. Only people knowing where to look would find the place."

"Thanks, Kiki. Having a plan B is always good."

"Brad, may I talk to Stephen?" asked Nick.

Nick heard a door opening.

"Hey, brother. What's up?" Stephen asked.

"We're working on this mess," responded Nick. "Brad says things aren't good."

They heard Stephen sigh. "We're coping. Brad is the only one going down the mountain. He feels that the less traffic, the smaller the chance we'll draw attention. We're shuttering the windows at night. The good news is we have lots of food."

Good, thought Nick. Brad was just being cautious, but still. "Stephen, I may be out of touch for a couple of weeks. Don't worry. Kiki and I are in good hands. Let me talk to Mom, please."

"Hi, Mom. Sounds like things are getting a little rough there."

"I'm not worried," she said.

Her voice sounded artificially cheerful to Nick. He didn't want her worrying about them. "Good. Kiki and I are helping from here. I'll call you within ten days. Hold those younguns together." She chuckled. "Bye bye. Love you all."

Nick hung up. Kiki watched him. "I'll be fine. They sound good."

"They did," she said. If only she were as sure as she sounded. "Things didn't sound good for Brad. Maybe we should get some news of what's going on back there."

"News would only make me worry. All of it's out of our hands." Nick stood. "I need to find Ron."

"If things get bad and they have to flee, at least we'll know to look for them at the ranch," she said as he left.

Chapter Twenty-Seven

September 22
Washington, D.C.

"Mr. President, our task force in Russia is ready. We need your approval," stated General Edwards.

"David, go through it again for me," said the president.

"Yes, sir. George Pickering should explain the first part."

The president looked at the thin face below his gleaming shaved head.

"Mr. President, NSA learned that the target we are after, Major Verenich, is vacationing in Sochi. We believe that is the destination of the convoy carrying the vaccine. He is overseeing the pickup and collecting the money. The intelligence we got from the suspect names him as the principle driver."

The president sat back in thought. "Do you know where the shipment is going from there, or who the buyer is?"

David Kennedy brushed gray locks from his brow. "Sir, that is information we hope to get from Verenich. Our capture team is on a ship in the Black Sea, next port of call Sochi. Our interrogation team is aboard, too."

"You're putting them at risk," stated the president.

"They volunteered, Mr. President. We flew them out yesterday with their equipment. This was the fastest way to extract the information we need."

"Whatever happens, take care of them. They weren't treated well the last time they worked for the government."

"Yes, sir. The secondary target on this mission is the shipment of vaccine. We will hijack it," said Kennedy. "We have a pirate team to catch it at sea."

"What's the worst that can happen?" asked the president.

General Edwards spoke in a low voice. "If our teams get busted, things could be real dicey on the political front."

"To say nothing of the captives," mused the president.

"Sir, in case of an emergency, we have USS Carl Vinson. We'll put tankers in the air from Turkey, so the F-18s can be there. We also plan to orbit stealth Predators for immediate help."

"And we'll keep all these forces hidden from the Russians how?"

"Sir, if the excrement hits the ventilator, we'll suppress and get our people out. Damn the costs."

The president smiled, nodding. "Best we can do. Go with it gentlemen." The president's mind wondered. If the hierarchy in Russia is involved, they wouldn't want any information to get out. The stakes were high for them. Yet they couldn't protest after the fact. Surprise and speed were prime. If things went wrong, were they worse off than now? The United States needed that vaccine. Predictions placed the causality rate at 10,000 per day if they couldn't get control. Reports had 3,000 dead from civil unrest, riots by any other name. The troops and law enforcement were scared. They weren't taking any chances.

The president visualized the United States as a giant wheel, hundreds of feet high. The economy and society kept it rotating. Small chinks knocked out of it had little effect. The inertia prevented any one thing from disrupting it. Attack the supports for that wheel, and it would come to a crashing halt. Electricity and the automated infrastructure were those supports. They had been damaged. Then the axel, people and their faith in the government was attacked with this bio-attack. There was a very real chance the wheel would crash. The United States would never be the same again. Just as the 9/11 attack changed life, this was that, magnified by a hundred times.

Chapter Twenty-Eight

September 24
The Black Sea Port, Sochi, Russia

The tramp freighter that Kiki and Nick were on was quite different from the FBI's luxury yacht they'd last used for interrogations. That was part of the disguise they'd been told by Lieutenant Toby Williams. Williams was the team leader on the raid to capture Verenich. Zyra had also volunteered for this mission. Speaking Russian like a native, she would direct.

With a blast from its horn, the ship approached the dock. They had exotic tropical fruits to unload. The crew appeared as slovenly as the ship and were ignored until late afternoon. The first customs official walked off with a bag of mangos, passion fruit, and a wad of cash in his pocket, waving for them to proceed unloading.

Under the cover of night, six people slipped from the ship to the abandoned pier. Nick and Kiki watched the shadows go. Nick nudged Kiki and pointed to the next pier. A new freighter, well lit, with Chinese markings was berthed. A stocky man in a black full-length leather coat was shaking hands with a man on board. He carried a satchel as he descended the gangplank. A black car waited on the dock.

Kiki nudged Nick. "Something's not right about that," she said, tilting her head toward the figures on the dock.

Nick looked around. Theirs was one of two ships docked tonight.

Zyra wore a form-fitting black mesh pantsuit. With six-inch heels, she stood out in any crowd, towering over everybody, a picture of intriguing and statuesque beauty. In the lobby of Verenich's hotel, heads turned. As she entered the bar, the buzz of conversation quieted. She sat at the end of the bar, alone.

Verenich entered the bar in a celebratory mood. He'd completed the largest deal in his life. All that remained was loading the special crates onto the waiting ship. That would be completed in the morning. The trucks were here. He noticed the very tall slender black woman at the bar.

Someone new. Her air of assurance drew him. He watched her reject another offer of free drinks. He would have her.

Easing onto the stool next to her, he placed the bag between his feet on the floor. She ignored him. The bartender set a vodka on the bar, having learned his tastes. "You are new here," stated Verenich. She gave him a cool look, appraising him, he knew. "Are you here on business or pleasure?" he asked.

"Some of both, I think," Zyra answered in faultless classic Russian. A faint smile creased her lips.

"Have you visited Sochi before?" asked Verenich.

"During the Olympics."

"Oh, as a visitor or a competitor?" he asked, with a smile.

"Does that line work with the other girls you meet here?" her lips curved up.

Verenich laughed aloud. "Caught," he admitted. "May I buy you a drink?"

"Don Julio gold tequila, neat," Zyra answered.

"Where does a woman, speaking as an aristocrat, learn to favor expensive tequila?" asked Verenich. "I'm not sure they have that here."

"The world is a very large place, if one gets out of Russia. They had it the last time I was here. I brought it. Have you tried Don Julio?"

Verenich laughed. What a fascinating woman. "No. I am a vodka man. I tried tequila once."

"Perhaps you should widen your perspective." She held up two fingers, signaling the bartender. He returned with two glasses and a bottle of Don Julio. They watched as he poured the golden liquor.

"Don't we need lime and salt, like in the movies," said Verenich, eyeing the glass.

"That is for garbage tequila. This is to be savored as a work of art." Zyra picked up the glass, indicating he should do the same. She held hers out. They touched glasses in a faint clink. "Do not throw this down as you do with your vodka. Take a small sip. Let it roll around in your mouth. Enjoy the taste."

He took a small sip. The flavor was magnificent, not the burning he expected. She looked at him, one eyebrow perfectly arched in a question.

"It's good, very good," he assured her.

"There are things to be enjoyed if one takes the time," she said, a twinkle in her eye.

"Have you eaten dinner yet?" He knew she hadn't. The dinner hour started late here. "Come. Have dinner with me. I know the best restaurant in Sochi."

She looked thoughtful. "Do I need to change?"

His eyes slid over her. "Whatever you wear will be perfect."

"Another line?" she asked, eyebrows raised. They both laughed.

Verenich rose. "I must go to my room before we leave. The restaurant is close. We can walk. Wait for me here," he commanded.

"Used to giving orders, are you? Maybe I will be here, maybe not." Zyra raised one eyebrow.

"I apologize for that tone. As you said, I am used to giving orders."

"Do you take them as well?" an impish look on her face.

Verenich fairly raced up the stairs to his second-floor suite, the money-laden bag banging against his leg. My God. What a woman! At the room, he stashed the bag under the bed. Tomorrow he'd put it in the hotel vault. In the bathroom, he looked himself over. A little water on his face, a little aftershave. He was ready. Verenich only took first or second floor suites.

He didn't have to wait for elevators, and there were emergency escapes through the windows, if needed. He'd learned that lesson the hard way.

Entering the lobby, he spotted the woman standing at the front window, gazing out. Every head was turned toward her. He touched her shoulder. "You never told me your name," he said, taking her arm.

"Zyra. And yours?"

"Dmitri," he said. Zyra was a head taller than he was. Rather than daunted by her stature, he took it as a challenge.

The walk was short, only a block. Though several people were waiting to be seated, they walked to reception. The tuxedoed man smiled, gestured to a waiter and motioned for Dmitri and Zyra to follow. In the candlelit room, heads turned, both men and women, their appraisals completely different.

"Do you think they have your tequila here?" he asked.

"I brought them a bottle, too."

Zyra gave the orders for the drinks, Dmitri ordered the meal. The waiter left. Zyra looked at Dmitri. "Are you here for business or pleasure?"

"Some of both, I hope," he said, looking at her with a slight smile at mimicking her.

"Do these lines come naturally or do you work at them?"

"Naturally."

Zyra rolled her eyes slightly, signaling a break in the wordplay. The waiter appeared, setting the drinks on the table. She picked hers up and held it out. Verenich touched her glass with his.

"Let's not talk of business. Tell me of yourself, early years." Zyra took a sip and leaned toward him.

"Not many women ask me that. My father was KGB, my mother upper class. I went to boarding schools and the military academy. Military intelligence, the Glavnoye Razvedyvatel'noye Upravleniye, wasn't for me, so I joined the KGB like my father. When the USSR broke up, I formed my own company."

Zyra held up a hand. "No later life. Were you happy as a child?" She tilted her head, a slight smile playing across her lips.

He took a sip of the liquor as he thought. Interesting. If she'd asked about his business, he'd be suspicious. She steered away from that. Childhood was a safe topic. "Happy? I studied hard, my father was my mentor. My life was strict. There wasn't time to be happy. I advanced."

"No time for a wife or family?" she purred and took another sip.

"It wasn't on my list of things to do. Until now, I haven't found anyone who I thought I...."

Zyra held up her hand. "Not another line, please."

He laughed. Whether it was the strange tequila or the success of the day or this woman, he didn't know. He was having a good time. For the first time he could remember, he felt no pressure to do something. Over their meal, he poured out his early life to her, his hopes of pleasing his father, of rising within the KGB. He had placed his grief of their death in a car wreck in a corner of his mind he rarely visited. He missed his mother. He hadn't told anyone that, ever. She listened to it all. He still talked to his father, but only in his mind since they died.

"One last tequila before we go?" she asked, signaling the waiter.

He nodded. As the drinks were delivered, he excused himself to go to the bathroom. Staring at his image in the bathroom mirror, he smiled. He really was having a good time. Whether they ended up in his room didn't matter. He wanted to see more of her.

Returning to the table, they toasted. "To a glorious evening," she said, holding up her glass. He agreed, clinking his to hers.

He was a little wobbly on the walk back. Must be the new drink, he reasoned.

"You need to get used to tequila. Perhaps I should walk you to your room," Zyra said. "That's to save you from another bad line."

That seemed so funny to him. He couldn't stop laughing. At his door, he fumbled with his key. She took it from him, opening the door. He entered. She followed, latching it behind her. He had to sit. The room was swimming before his eyes. She helped him to the couch. He barely made it.

Chapter Twenty-Nine

September 24
The Situation Room,
Washington, D.C.

The live-streaming video from the helicopter above the Rose Bowl was like a refugee documentary from a third world country. Tents covered the floor, people meandered around the makeshift city. The tiers were checker-boarded with plastic sheets used for shelter covering those huddled beneath. Lines of bedraggled figures snaked from the arena exits to the medical facilities now in the concession mezzanine underneath the stands.

Looking from the monitor to his Secretary of the Interior, Ron Carson, the president asked, "How many people are in there?"

"Seventeen thousand as of this morning," said Ron. "They are people whose homes burned in the riots last week, homeless from the streets, and those from areas near quarantine sites. We are screening to keep infection out. Thus far, we've been successful. Inevitably, we will miss someone and this will become another quarantine site."

"How many of these shelters are in Los Angeles now?"

"Twenty-two, with eight more being readied at this time. In addition, we have food and water distribution sites spread over the city and surrounding areas."

The president shook his head. "What has become of this country? In less than a month we've descended to third-world. How many quarantine sites in the Los Angeles area?"

The view on the monitor changed to Dr. Joel Albertson. Deep lines crossed his face, testament to sleepless nights. "Mr. President, we have seventeen with several hospitals completely converted to treatment and quarantine sites. It's similar in the other cities hit by the attack. Nationally, there are 154 sites operating with more being prepared."

"What's the fatality rate?" the president asked. His shoulders slumped, head down as if awaiting a blow.

"We're seeing 70,000 a month and still rising. The lack of vaccine is literally killing us. Producers assure us they are working as fast as they can to start up production lines."

In a quiet voice, the president said, "So at present, we are not even close to getting a handle on this." His voice rose. "I must inform you gentlemen that our trading partners are enacting a plan to quarantine the United States. There have been isolated cases in other countries, but nothing like the epidemic we are seeing."

There was a babble of voices at this news. The president held up a hand for silence. "I cannot blame them. We've received notice that no flights, ships, or visitors from the United States will be allowed. The European Union is asking for help with a blockade. All trade will cease. We will do the same on the west coast. I need not tell you what a disaster this is to our economy."

"Sir, when will this blockade be in place?" asked Secretary of State Sharon Volgyi.

The president looked at each of those present and the monitors showing those attending via teleconference. "I am in agreement with the necessity for a quarantine. We cannot export this disease. Our own military will begin the blockade tomorrow as part of their defensive patrolling. We are putting Border Patrol on notice they are to allow no one to cross the border into either Mexico or Canada. Deadly force is authorized."

"Surely we can decontaminate manufactured products," said Secretary Volgyi. "I would like to investigate ways for us to export goods assuring they are not contaminated,"

"Dr. Albertson, submit a list of those to help formulate a plan? Sharon, get with the Commerce Department and put something together."

All rose as the president stood. "Thank you, ladies and gentlemen. Ron, would you and General Edwards meet me in the Oval Office."

With the door closed, the president asked, "Where are we on the Russian mission?"

"Sir," began Ron Carson, "we have the suspect in custody. Our ship left port two hours ago. Verenich is being prepped for interrogation."

"And the second phase?"

David Kennedy spoke. "The Chinese ship carrying the vaccine is preparing to leave port. We will take her tomorrow night. Our team will act like typical pirates, demanding a ransom. Once it is paid, we will return the ship without the vaccine. They cannot protest the loss of a cargo that they deny exists."

The president nodded. "David, I want you to formulate a plan to buy the vaccine from Koltsovo. Do it under cover of another organization, not the U. S. If we cannot do that, we want people at the facility to change their minds."

Kennedy's eyebrows rose. This was a bold idea.

"Investigate who was receiving the vaccine. Somebody has a reason to immunize their people. I want to know who, and ultimately why. Ron, keep me up to date on the interrogation. Gentlemen, we are going to retaliate. Nobody fucks the United States of America and gets away with it."

Chapter Thirty

September 25
Sochi, Russia

Nick and Kiki eased the unconscious Major Dmitri Verenich into the isolation chamber. This cabin was not as finely outfitted as their stateroom aboard the boat. The walls were gray-painted steel, the floor steel plate. The one small porthole was painted over. Lights hung from bare fixtures in the ceiling. Zyra watched as IVs were inserted and attached to the sensors. Kiki marveled at the change in Zyra's appearance of a few hours ago, from statuesque beauty to hardened soldier in loose-fitting black coveralls. She had done a marvelous job of not only securing the subject, but getting information to use. Zyra was all business now.

The three sat as Nick adjusted drips and meds. "Let's wake him up," he said.

Kiki watched Nick and Zyra as Verenich first asked where he was, and then started yelling, seeking any sensory input from his body to his brain. The sound-deadening system didn't even allow him to hear his own cries.

"Dmi, I've been waiting for you," said Zyra, translating Nick's statement.

Dmitri heard the atonal words through the bone microphone. "Who is that?" he asked. "Only my father and mother called me that. They died two years ago in a car wreck."

"Nice of you to remember, son. And you couldn't be bothered to come to your father's funeral."

"I was tied up in something. I couldn't get away."

"Dmi, remember how I used to beat you for lying so badly. You got much better at it, but you could never lie to me and get away with it. You were doing something you thought more important, right?"

"I was."

"And here you are with me. That's not strange to you?"

"As you know, I've talked to you in my mind sometimes. This is the clearest I've ever heard you. Why can't I feel or see anything?"

Nick watched his vital signs rise. He was going to panic. Nick tweaked the sedatives.

"Your mother told you to find a good woman but you couldn't be bothered. The woman who so infatuated you gave you poison. So this is how you end up."

"I am dead?" His voice quavered.

"Struck down in the prime of your life by lust. Stop your sniveling. If I could, I would cuff you again for being so stupid. At least now I have someone to talk to."

"You would like what I built. After the breakup, I started my own army, small, but we did good work. Made money. This last deal was the best. I made a bargain with the director of this laboratory to sell things they produced."

"What kind of things?"

"Biological. These Chinese bought virus agents from me, then hired my boys to deliver it. After that, they bought the serums against that virus."

"How did you keep the government thugs from finding out?"

"I didn't. I paid them off. We were all in it together, making millions of rubles."

"And then you got stupid. What's going to happen now?"

"My boy Sergei will take over. He knows how."

"Is that the Sergei who lived down the street from us?"

"No, this is Sergei Kuzmich. He worked with me at KGB."

"We have nothing but time. Tell me about your rise in KGB and how you built your army."

Kiki left. On deck, the breeze revitalized her as the ship crossed the Black Sea. A few other boats could be seen, but none were close. Once again, she was amazed at how Nick found the one key that opened these peoples' minds, led them to tell everything.

They would all be glad when they were away from the Russian sphere. She suspected this would be only a temporary departure. There were other tasks to do in Russia.

Chapter Thirty-One

September 25
Casa Grande, Arizona

Sheriff Brad Tierman looked through the chain-link fence surrounding the rodeo grounds. People milled about, ducking in and out of tents. California refugees had made it to Casa Grande. A few stared back at him, faces blank or pleading. He walked to another fenced area. It was the medical area filled with tents, red crosses painted on the tops. A tank crouched at one corner, another at the diagonal corner. Their guns were not pointed out. With the refugees had come smallpox. These camps were the last attempt to keep the disease out of his city. Brad nodded at several National Guard troops patrolling the perimeter.

"Good morning, Captain Smith," he said at the headquarters office. The room was typical military, gray metal desks, gray metal filing cabinets, gray desk lamps, a picture of President Donaldson on the wall, flanked by the American flag.

"Morning, Sheriff." The slim black officer stood to shake hands as Brad entered.

"How are things here on the front lines?" Brad asked, taking the offered hand.

"Not as good as yesterday. More people, more cases of sickness. Our screening has kept the infected out of the general population, but it is only temporary."

"How are your soldiers holding up?"

"Following orders, but they're worried about friends and family. So am I. The understanding that this duty is protecting their folks holds 'em here, but they don't like it much. Last night, we had to use a cattle prod on a twelve-year-old climbing the fence."

Brad stared at him, picturing the scene. It could have been one of his kids. "Kobe, I'm trying to hold things together in the city, too. I'm seeing high-school friends, people I grew up with, in groups demanding food and water. We're doing what we can. I feel the rising tension. When the riot starts, we'll be shooting people we know. And it will start. If smallpox shows up in the city, we'll be in real trouble."

"Any word on a vaccination program?" The captain's face was lined from fatigue.

"It's coming, but no dates."

"Yeah, the same with me. No dates for any relief either." The sounds of the camp were a background murmur in the silence that followed.

Brad nodded understanding. "I know. My deputies are working twelve-hour shifts, no days off for weeks. No end in sight. Things are worse in Phoenix. Riot-caused fires have burned major parts of the city. The casualties rate from these is over 1000, many shot. So far, we've avoided that. The Maricopa Sheriff's Department is asking for help. I don't have any to give."

"At least you can turn down the request. I have to follow orders. My people would refuse to leave this area where their families are. What do I do then?" Kobe shook his head.

"I'm going to start deputizing volunteers tomorrow. We need more manpower. If it works out, I might be able to give you some relief here."

"Thanks. That'll help."

Brad walked back to his car. He was bone tired from lack of sleep, stress over deploying his men, trying to keep a lid on the unrest, and dissatisfaction with the government response. The more he thought about deputizing volunteers, the more he liked the idea. It would involve the people in keeping law and order in place.

At the office, he called his chief deputy in and they talked the idea over. Volunteers would not be paid, but they and their families would get supplies – food, water, fuel, whatever the department could spare. They and their families would get first inoculations when they arrived.

He would go over the plan with the rest of the department. Deputies would submit a list of people they trusted. They'd cull that list to ten to see how the program worked. It would be OJT, on the job training, pairing up volunteers with deputies. They didn't have time or people to start a training program.

If nothing else, this plan was an offensive step in taking control. To date all efforts were defensive.

The department meeting was well received. In two days, names in hand, Brad and his chief deputy would approach potential volunteers before the end of the week.

For the first time Brad felt optimistic as he climbed the driveway to the Sabino house, When he told Nick's brother, Stephen, of his plans, he immediately volunteered.

Chapter Thirty-Two

September 26
Democratic People's Republic of Korea

Lieutenant Gun Rahn looked over the shoulder of Sergeant Kwang Ryang. Scrolling down the screen were thousands of internet viruses. This flood would damage the internet for weeks. This was phase two of the North Korean attack on imperialist America.

Their hack into America's electrical grid control system had ended. The Americans had blocked them, but their grid was damaged, areas blacked out for months or more. The orders and prices for replacement parts from China, had skyrocketed. The People's Republic of China would share the profits with the Democratic People's Republic of Korea.

Gun tapped Kwang on the shoulder. He pressed the enter key. Nothing happened. Kwang looked up. Something was wrong. Kwang repeated the commands. Nothing.

"Find out what's blocking us," commanded Gun. "I'll get you help." He instructed several techs to work with Kwang. Gun went to his office to report this snag.

"It is expected," said Captain Han-jae. "The Americans blocked our internet access. Our allies provided us a workaround." He handed Gun a thumb drive. "We needed to try our own access to see how fast the Americans were moving to stop us. Now, let's hit them."

Gun handed Kwang the thumb drive. Only one file was on it. A click and it started installing. When done, Kwang clicked on his browser. They were in! Again, Kwang brought up the virus files. A few clicks later, sent appeared.

Chapter Thirty-Three

September 26
The Situation Room,
Washington, D.C.

"Gentlemen and ladies, we need to get the latest updates and make plans," said the president to his crisis team. "George, start us off."

"Mr. President, we are now sure the North Koreans hacked our systems," said George Pickering. "NSA set up a trap. We blocked North Korea's access to the internet. They came in on a workaround. The tracks were the same as the first attempt."

"Good job, George." President Donaldson gazed out the windows of the conference room. He turned to General Edwards. "Let's get some ideas how we're going to retaliate for this cyber attack. Everything except nukes is on the table."

Pickering nodded acknowledgement of the compliment. "I'll get a taskforce together today. We'll have something for you tomorrow." He smiled at the rare victory.

"Mr. President, we found out something else. The workaround came in through China. We believe they are involved in this attack."

The president was silent. "Ladies and gentlemen, we need to brainstorm. I need open minds and unfiltered ideas. Let me summarize what we know of the bio-attack first. Our latest intelligence indicates it was a hired job. This attack appears to have been done under the sanction of Russian authorities, but not by them directly. The source of the pathogen was a Russian laboratory. The CDC matched the genetic signature to the strains at Koltsovo. A rogue gang coerced someone at the Vector Institute to obtain the virus. We haven't pinpointed who yet. David, does the CIA have anything to add?"

"The director was coerced to begin vaccine production, a seemingly innocuous task. Vaccine production against this strain began months ago with the first shipment departing from the Russian port of Sochi on a Chinese ship. We don't know that the destination is China, but somebody wants their people vaccinated."

"Mr. President, are we assuming that China is behind this bio-attack?" asked Secretary of State Volgyi.

"It's too early to fix on that assumption," said the president. "But there appears to be a Chinese connection, whether official or rogue. The same for Russia. Russia is capable of acting out of revenge, and we hurt their economy badly. People in charge blame us for the breakup of the USSR, and they have long memories. Though they may not be behind the attack, certain members of the government turned a blind eye to it."

"Mr. President, the U. S. is China's biggest trading partner. What possible reason would they have to destroy that?" asked Volgyi.

Ron Carson spoke up. "Let's assume the U. S. is not the biggest trading partner for the moment. China wants to dominate global economics. They want oil traded in yuan, not dollars. They want to control commerce. In the world today, the land area under your political control is no longer the measure of power. It's the economy."

The president nodded at Ron Carson.

Carson continued. "Rather than overtake the U. S. economy, the events of the last month knocked the dominant economy from the map. We have yet to see what the plan is to replace the trade with the U. S. If they are behind this, they must have one."

Secretary of State Volgyi spoke up again. "One thing the Chinese learned over the last two thousand years is that their true enemy is an unsatisfied Chinese population. That will bring them down."

"Exploring that reasoning," said General Edwards, "how do they prevent an unsatisfied population? Unsatisfied means out of work and hungry. But maybe we need to focus on the definition of population for a moment. If ten percent were unsatisfied, would that be a problem?"

President Donaldson watched his people. Good session, he thought.

"The brutality of the government would not find ten percent beyond their ability to control," said Volgyi.

"I think we must assume that ten percent unrest where it is dispersed would not be a problem." said the president. "They know how to control isolated dissent. But if there were concentrated pockets of high dissent, that would be trouble. Those pockets could grow and spread. They would have to be dealt with." He looked around the table. Several people nodded agreement.

"If the number of those pockets were great enough, it would strain the ability of the police and military to control them," said Edwards. "Plagues in those areas would do nicely. Only those deserving and required would get the vaccine."

There was dead silence around the table. The concept was monstrous.

Chapter Thirty-Four

September 29
The Black Sea

The voyage across the Black Sea and through the straights had been uneventful. It had given Nick and Zyra time to open Verenich's mind fully. Kiki sat in for a while. Old memories surfaced. Her abhorrence of ripping apart people's minds had seared her before. Despite their actions and her team's cause, it still hurt. They were now in the Mediterranean Sea. Satellite photos showed the Chinese ship had entered. Once their route was determined, the hijack would be set up.

On deck, Kiki watched the SEAL hijack team prepare for their attack. Satellite communication placed the Chinese freighter fifteen miles away. The three Zodiac inflatable rafts were painted like old Syrian military boats.

The team wore civilian clothes, disguising themselves as former Syrian military deserters. Their weapons were AK-47 style, with RPGs. Their direction of attack would be from the Syrian coast. In reality, our old freighter was to be the incognito mother ship.

Kiki attended the planning and briefing session. Two boats would attack at speed, threatening to hole the ship with the RPGs. The third boat would stand off at a distance with suppressing fire if the Chinese crew resisted. The third boat also had jamming equipment to keep the ship from radioing for help.

Kiki asked if she could go on the third boat, lend some assistance. The refusal froze in Lieutenant Mendez's throat when he recognized her from Afghanistan. She had provided suppressing fire at a particularly tough town that was an ambush in disguise. She saved a lot of lives that day.

"It would be an honor to have you as part of the team. Sergeant, got anything the Iblis can use?" he said, using the name the ragheads had given her. It was an honor to be so feared by your enemies.

She glanced at Nick. He looked worried. "I'll be in good hands, Nick." The burly sergeant handed her a scope-mounted long-barreled AR-10.

"My personal reach out and touch someone rifle," he said. "It's in 25-06. Long range, low recoil so it stays on target."

"I'll take good care of it," said Kiki. She cradled the rifle, feeling its heft and balance. It seemed to fit her.

The Zodiac boat ride took forty-five minutes before the two attack boats approached. With Syrian flags, the Chinese crew assumed they were military allies. From 700 yards away, Kiki watched through the twelve-power scope. Only when the two boats were 200 yards away did the crew realize they were under attack. Behind her, the radioman jammed the freighter's radio distress call.

Two uniformed men appeared on the upper deck with machineguns and began shooting at the boats. She placed the crosshairs on one man, squeezed the trigger. There was barely any recoil. The man tumbled over the railing, falling to the deck below. Christ, that bullet got there fast! she thought as her sights centered on the second man. His hands went into the air, gun falling to the deck. She held him in the crosshairs as the first of the team came over the railing, guns up.

The team fanned out in pairs, rounding up the crew. Thirty minutes later, the radioman told her everything was secured, the crew locked up. He sent a message to their freighter as they started back.

She climbed over the railing into Nick's waiting arms. "I'm okay, Nick it went well. We got the ship." She had felt good in the sniper role, something she knew, something she did well.

"I know, I heard the message. The new crew is leaving to take over." He pointed to a group of men getting on the boat she'd returned in. They would sail the Chinese ship to an Israeli port where it would be hidden during ransom negotiations. The vaccine would be off-loaded for transport to the U.S.

"Is Major Verenich going with the vaccine?" she asked.

"Yeah. They don't yet understand what shape he's in. Faced with the real world of not being dead, being a captive, he will retreat back into the existence of living with his dead father."

Kiki felt a tingling in her mind like when her arm went to sleep. She shivered. Oh no, she thought.

"Nicely done, Nick and Katherine. The rumors of what you are doing is circulating among the crew. They are in a state between awe and revulsion. Neither emotion is to my taste, but the other ship has enough fear and hatred by the Chinese crew to feed me."

Jesus, they didn't need a visit from this Director again. Revulsion rose in her like sour bile. The idea of it guiding people to war with fear and hatred so it could feed on those emotions disgusted her. "Nick, we can't deal with this creature now." She struggled to tamp down her hatred for it lest she give him sustenance.

"Katherine, I have missed you and Nick. You are the only ones of your race I communicate with. I do so enjoy our chats. You have learned to control your fear and hatred and no longer are a source of food for me. Maybe that is why I enjoy you. You are aware of me and you do create tasty meals for me. I will say that this latest conflict lacks the hot spicy flavor of the religious wars. That blind hatred does not

contain the taint of envy arising now in your enemies."

"Envy?" asked Nick. They've always been envious. Why more so now?

"Oh yes. Your enemies are driven by the desire for what you have. They want to control you; they want your position in the world. Now they feel they have the opportunity and will take it by destroying your nation. It is already under way, as you know. Your nation will retaliate, creating a feast for me. Your world is changing. Must go."

Like a soda gone flat, the prickling sensation was gone. Thank God, Kiki thought. "Destroy our nation, retaliation? This sounds like nuclear holocaust. Nick, I'm worried." Her voice trembled.

"Me, too. One thing this creature said that is true is the United States we go back to will be different. The status from Brad tells us that," added quietly.

"Are we going back to the U. S. now?" she asked, her voice hopeful.

"All our information was sent. We'll see what comes back."

I doubt we'll be returning to the U. S. anytime soon, Kiki thought. She wrapped her arms around herself. She had never missed home so much.

Chapter Thirty-Five

September 30
Situation Room,
Washington, D.C.

"Ladies and gentlemen, we have two topics to discuss today," said the president. "First, we have confirmed the cyber attack is from North Korea. As part of that investigation, we uncovered a link to China. Our thoughts as of now are that North Korea hacked into our electrical grid controls with the help of China.

"After the latest sanctions, North Korea has plenty of motive to attack us, but we are puzzled by China's assistance in this attack. Thoughts?"

"I see two purposes in China's moves," said Ron Carson. "The cyber attack weakened us. With the quarantine of the United States cutting off trade, we no longer are an economic power. We are also buying billions of dollars of equipment from them. It is a win-win situation from their standpoint. They come out looking good by helping us while inflating prices to astronomical levels."

"There may be another reason," said George Pickering. "We suspect a Trojan is built into the control hardware we are getting from them. They may be able to gain control of the system at some time in the future. Along with Israel, we did that to the Iranians to sabotage their nuclear weapons program years ago."

The president looked at the grim faces around the table. Potential bad news on top of bad news. "George, initiate a program to assure our system won't be compromised in the future. We have to know our grid system will hold up."

"Yes, Mr. President."

"The other topic for today has to do with the bio-attack. David, bring us up to date."

"Our interrogation thus far reveals complicity by Russian officials, though we have not tied it to sanctioned government involvement. There is also potential Chinese involvement with the ship of Chinese registry transporting the vaccine."

"The question is what to do with this information?" said the president.

"We have to retaliate, sir," said General Edwards.

"Of course you are right. But how?"

"We can bomb them into oblivion," barked the general.

"Yes, Tom there is always that. Dave, George, how long before you can identify those behind these attacks with certainty?"

George ran his hand over his head. "We're working as fast as we can, but any tie to the Chinese government is convoluted."

"Tom, George, David, start working on retaliation plans. George, David, get me the plans for acquiring more vaccine from Koltsovo. The shipment we hijacked will be on a C-17 immediately after it docks. We'll distribute the hijacked vaccine as soon as it arrives. We need more until our own production catches up. David, we need to know if the Chinese involvement is official. Sharon, what's your take on the Russians?"

"Mr. President, NATO has been weakened by our domestic problems. We're seeing a buildup of Russian forces in the western sectors. After their success in Ukraine, they are emboldened by the deteriorating strength of the European Union. Border countries are reporting more unrest from Russian ethnic groups. It is the same model used in Ukraine. NATO cannot resist an attack with conventional forces, and we don't believe Russia has removed nuclear weapons from the table in blocking any counterattack."

"Tom, do you agree?"

"Yes, sir." Edwards wore a grim look. "The Russians are positioning for a soft invasion in Latvia and Lithuania. Poland will be next. Our NATO Rapid Strike Force is a surgical response. It will only be effective if it is employed quickly and followed up by NATO or UN troops. The RSF does not have the strength to prevail in a long campaign."

"Sharon, what's the political attitude in Europe?"

"The EU is seeking assurances that NATO is capable of protecting them. We are not in a position to back NATO."

The president looked at Elizabeth Gutierrez and Robert Chou, the two Congressional leaders. "I may need to call an emergency session on a moment's notice. Please notify members of that." They both nodded.

"Sharon, keep tabs open where aid to the EU may come from. See who's offering help, what kind, and in a position to do so. Find out what the quid pro quo is."

"Yes, Mr. President."

Chapter Thirty-Six

October 2
Casa Grande, Arizona

"Hey, Nick when are you coming back?" asked Brad, talking into the speakerphone. He looked out the sliding glass door across the patio toward the setting sun. His position as Sheriff had been a nightmare these last weeks.

"Probably not for a while. Can't say where we are or what we're doing, but we are working on the problems you are facing." He looked around the drab cabin that was their meeting room. How he longed for the wide-open spaces and blue skies of Arizona.

"Yeah, I understand how that goes. Whatever you're doing, thanks."

"How are things at home?" asked Nick. He was concerned. News of conditions in the U. S. wass hard to come by.

"The first cases of smallpox appeared at an urgent care facility in Casa Grande a week ago. The patients were relatives of long-time residents. Fleeing San Diego, they had slipped past the blockade. The hospital went into quarantine mode immediately. The care facility was closed for decontamination. We erected a temporary chain-link fence around the house of the Casa Grande family. The fence was for show so that people would know the Sheriff's Department was on top of the problem."

Smallpox in Casa Grande! That was a worry. "Is everybody at our house okay?"

"Yeah, thanks for the vaccine. Don't know how you did it. Nobody other than the troops and law enforcement have been vaccinated so far."

"You're welcome. How's my family doing?"

"They're doing well. We initiated a volunteer program because we were so shorthanded. Steve and Barb volunteered immediately. We put them in charge of the kitchen supplying meals to the refugees and those families housebound. Some of them never ate so good."

"That's great to hear." Nick could hear pride in Brad's voice.

"Our program has become a model for other departments. By involving the people, we've had no demonstrations or riots like Phoenix or Los Angeles. It's given us a sense of community this country lost."

"You said refugees. You have refugees?" Were things so bad people were fleeing their homes? Nick felt helpless. He was half a world away and could do nothing for his family.

"Yeah. There's a blockade on I-8 at Gila Bend to keep those escaping the quarantine in California from bringing the plague east. We've been able to contain them, almost. We're seeing refugees here in Casa Grande. Once they stay in Gila Bend for the gestation period without showing signs of smallpox, they can continue east. Some of those people never saw a tractor and thought milk came from a carton. We've put them to work on the farms."

"Wow, quite a program."

"Yeah, I saw too many documentaries of refugee camps with people doing nothing but figuring what they should be given next. How's Kiki doing?"

"She's doing well." Nick counted his blessing having her with him.

"Have you got power back?" he asked.

"Mostly. We still have blackouts, but they're scheduled so we can prepare. You want to talk to your mother?"

"Yeah, thanks."

"Nick, is that you?" Her voice quavered a little.

"It's me, Mom. How are you doing?" She sounded tired.

"I'm doing fine. All this trouble is keeping me busy. I'm taking care of the kids while Stephen and Barb fix meals. It's tiring, but I'm home-schooling them and thinking of working at the elementary school to get it started again. Can't have these kids just sitting around. There's lots of children in the camps, too."

"Mom, watch yourself. Don't take on too much."

"I'll be fine. Where are you? Is Kiki with you?"

"I'm not allowed to say where we are, but yes, Kiki is with me. We're both doing fine."

"Okay, you take care of that girl. I think she's special."

"So do I, Mom."

"Brad wants to speak with you again. Bye, son. Talk to you again soon. Love you."

"Love you back, Mom."

"Hey, Nick, I forgot to tell you I ran into a friend of yours. He's a detective from Albuquerque, Johnny Cano. Says he ran across you and Kiki a couple of years ago on a murder and drug smuggling case."

Nick froze. "I remember the name, but never met him. Don't believe anything he says." How much did Cano know about the terrorist fight, what he and Kiki did?

"It's all good, Nick. He says you and Kiki saved a cop's life and took out some local Albuquerque low-lifes. He's working for me now. Quit the Albuquerque PD a few months ago. Raised in Casa Grande, he returned here. He's a natural fit with us."

"Okay, maybe I'll get to meet him face-to-face when Kiki and I get home."

"Yeah, says he wants to buy the both of you a beer, so hurry back."

"Be there when we can, Thanks for taking care of everyone there. Talk you later." Nick hung up and stared at the gray steel wall. He felt trapped in a place he didn't want to be, but doing something he had to do.

Chapter Thirty-Seven

October 2
Mediterranean Sea

Secretary Ron Carson's voice came over the secure video conference board. "Nick, Katherine, Zyra, we need you to return to Russia," Kiki's stomach tightened. They were in the interrogation room on board the disguised ship. Ron continued, "Our vaccine production is slowly building, but the United States is losing 40,000 people a day to this disease. That rate continues to grow. The vaccine we hijacked will help, but it's a tiny fraction of what is needed. We want you to become the buyer of vaccine. That means contacting those in charge of production and offering them more money than their other customer."

"Why us?" asked Kiki. "That's out of our area of expertise."

"Not entirely. Zyra's fluent in Russian. We also want you to interrogate another person. We're going to team the three of you up with an experienced agent. A luxury yacht will meet you tomorrow. We'll move your equipment onto it. I'm sending you the mission files now."

"Ron, we're not CIA field agents." Kiki looked at Nick. He was nodding. Zyra was impassive. "This is extremely dangerous."

"If we had another choice, we'd take it. This new agent, Sasha Belikova, is familiar with the area."

Zyra's normally impassive face had a smile, or at least that's what Kiki thought it was.

"I will explain Sasha to Nick and Katherine," said Zyra. "She is known to me."

"She is on the boat heading for you now," said Ron. "I'm sending files explaining the mission. I'll call you tomorrow after you've had a chance to look over the information." The screen went dark.

Nick and Kiki turned toward Zyra.

"Sasha and I are what you call girlfriends. We know each other since youth in Russia. Together, we escape and go to Israel, became agents for our government. We are good team. We fight against the *ublyudki*," she snarled, "the bastards who have our homeland. In this fight we are allies."

Again, Zyra smiled. "Sasha is skier, Olympic alternate in Sochi Olympics. We will be fine in mission."

I sure hope so, thought Nick as he logged onto the laptop and downloaded the mission files. He was nervous. The thought that he and Kiki would go back to Russia was a dark cloud in his mind. They gathered around the monitor to review them.

"Our cover with port authorities is late season tourists," noted Kiki, "but also representatives of World Games Winter Sports looking at Sochi as a site."

Nick pointed at the monitor, reading further. "The crew on the yacht will be the SEAL team members who hijacked the Chinese freighter. The ransom demand has been sent to the owners. The hijackers are demanding twenty million dollars for the return of the ship and crew. So far no response."

"They are trying to find it," stated Zyra. "The crew sailing it now have disguised it, changed the registry and put props on the deck. They will not discover it."

Kiki continued to read the files over Nick's shoulder. "After the ship docks at Haifa, the vaccine will fly out, along with Major Verenich, as we expected. As part of this new mission, we're being met tonight to transfer to the yacht. Obviously, the request for our help wasn't a request," bitterness in her voice as she remembered the last time they were shanghaied.

"I know, K," said Nick, "but this time, I see the necessity. Mortality rates of 40,000 innocents a day is reason enough for me."

"You're right, Nick. I just wish the asking weren't such a pretense."

"K, if not us, then who?"

"All right, I'm over it. Let's get on with this mission." She continued to read aloud. "Our first contact will be with Verenich's second-in-command, Sergei Kuzmich. We will set up a deal with him to buy the next vaccine shipment. That sounds simple enough."

"It is rarely so," said Zyra. "We are dealing with devils." Her eyes glowed. "There will be traps within traps."

Chapter Thirty-Eight

October 2
Situation Room,
Washington, D.C.

"Mr. President, we have initiated our program to acquire vaccine from Koltsovo," said Ron Carson. "Personnel will be on the way tomorrow. We will offer the gang selling the vaccine a deal."

"And if they refuse?" asked the president.

"The offer will be double what the previous customer was paying. It will be difficult for them to turn down. If they do, we have contingency plans, sir."

"If they do, it is because of other pressures," said Secretary of State Sharon Volgyi. "To me, sir, that will be the strongest indication of government involvement, either Chinese,

Russian or both. How far are we willing to go in that case?"

"Something to think about," mused the president.

"There is another wrinkle," said General Edwards. "Mr. President, after the last session, we intensified our monitoring of Russian and Chinese satellites. Since the ransom demand, both countries re-tasked observation satellites to search for the hijacked ship. The governments are talking."

"Mr. President," said Secretary of State Sharon Volgyi, "to be fair, we have also been asked to search for the hijacked ship. We provided satellite photos showing the hijacking boats approaching the ship, but the satellite moved out of position soon after. We have not picked up that ship since."

"Are we that incompetent? I think not. In other words," said the president, "Chinese/Russian governmental collusion is not proved."

"No, sir," conceded General Edwards. "But we have not been asked to re-task satellites for the search."

"So, the possibility the suppliers of the vaccine are not a private company, is greater. We will require another plan, one designed to bypass the government. A much more difficult mission," the president murmured.

"Yes, sir, the next ship will be heavily guarded, unless we take possession at the port. If we do, it will be our ship in danger of hijack," said Edwards.

"What arrangements have you made to protect it?" asked the president.

"The transport freighter is a Navy ship in disguise," informed General Edwards. "It has a full compliment of military grade controls and instrumentation, along with armaments. It's equipped with a high-speed propulsion system making it capable of outrunning anything other than military ships. It will take more than a contingent of pirate craft to take her."

"The response to our offer to become the customer will be telling," said Secretary Volgyi. "Our agents must be able to read the situation. Gangs are notoriously untruthful."

"And dangerous," added the president. "Perhaps we should discuss Plan B."

"Sir, are we willing to put military presence in Russia?" asked General Edwards.

"Tell me exactly what you are thinking."

"Mr. President, we believe the shipments were going through Sochi to disguise the final destination, China. There are overland routes through Kazakhstan, or Novokuznetsk. Shorter, but they carry risks of bandits or rebels. Troop presence would be required to guard those shipments. That would be overt government support. In addition, the Chinese would have to provide troop protection. Western China can be rough, too. If they perceive that the sea routes are in jeopardy, they may change to land routes."

The president frowned.

The general continued, "Getting to those shipments would require forces on the ground. That would be 2000 miles from friendly territory. The other nightmare is getting the shipment out of Russian or China if we are able to secure it. Logistics would be a nightmare."

"What you're telling me is that we may be able to secure only one more shipment, if we cannot make a deal with the gang supplying it,"

"I'm afraid so, Mr. President."

"Ron, make the deal. Cost is not the issue."

Chapter Thirty-Nine

October 4
The Black Sea, Port Sochi

Once again, Kiki, Zyra and Nick were on a luxury yacht – lavish staterooms, three decks, the top an observation platform complete with telescope. Sasha Belikova and her brother, Ilia Belikov, had arrived by helicopter the day before. Unlike Zyra, Sasha was short, compact and muscular. Short brown hair framed her pale round face. She wore the same intense expression as Zyra, except when she smiled.

Ilia was small, a former gymnast, with broad shoulders and narrow waist and hips. Blond hair accentuated his piercing blue eyes. He walked with a bounce in his step, while Sasha seemed to glide.

Sitting in the main cabin, they were smiling. Whoever owned this yacht was beyond rich. The walls were teak, the floor mosaic tile. A chandelier hung over the massive table, its crystal prisms spreading rainbow colors across the walls. Sasha described Sochi as a resident would.

"After the Olympics, I stayed in Sochi, running a ski accessory shop while working undercover for Israel. It has given me the opportunity to become acquainted with people and politics in Sochi. I made arrangements with the mayor to take you to tour the ski facilities, explaining that we are considering holding World Winter Championships in Sochi in one year. We will get the royal treatment." Sasha smiled.

"But won't they check to see if we do represent the World Sports Organization?" asked Kiki.

"We are not representing them. We are representing a powerful commercial sponsor, who must remain anonymous. We cannot be seen to influence the board of directors. The mayor understands completely. We will also be looking at buying accommodations, hotels, restaurants, even the cab company, whatever will make money." Again, Sasha smiled. "The mayor has a list."

"How do we contact Sergei Kuzmich and the gang supplying smallpox vaccine?" asked Nick.

"Ilia can answer that," said Sasha. "He's been in Novosibirsk for two years working for your CIA."

Ilia smiled. "My contacts located him here in Sochi at the same hotel where Major Verenich was staying. We have a suite there. Apparently, he's looking into Major Verenich's disappearance, though it seems not so diligently. We circulated a rumor he was killed by a prisoner he once tortured. I don't think Kuzmich is very concerned."

"We'll be working from the suite?" asked Nick.

"It gives us an easy base, minutes from everywhere. Do not worry, our SEAL team is ten minutes away if we need them."

"Go dress in your finery," said Sasha. "We meet the mayor in one hour. Zyra dear, I'm sorry you must stay. Someone will remember you were with Verenich the night he disappeared. You don't blend well in Sochi."

Kiki felt uncomfortable in the slitted black leather skirt and low-cut top. Her four-inch heels completed her discomfort. She wasn't used to dressing like this. She looked at Nick. He smiled and whistled. In his black slacks and black silk shirt, he looked like a movie star. Ilia wore a tailored black suit with iridescent blue silk tie. He could step into any elegant scene. He looked hot.

Sasha wore a tight-fitting stretch suit. Its iridescent blue matched Ilia's tie. Gold earrings with blue diamonds adorned her ears. Four-inch heels topped her out at five-foot eight inches.

They got appreciative stares during the short walk from the hotel to the restaurant. She knew this one well, the second best restaurant in Sochi. As the concierge greeted them, the mayor arrived. The seating was elegant, and the mayor's presence ensured several of the wait-staff continuously hovered to meet any need. Sasha did most of the talking in Russian after the introductions. The mayor's consumption of vodka was astonishing as he envisioned another grand event in Sochi. Several times, Sasha poured her vodka into the water glass. At last, the evening wound down, and until tomorrows were said. The four of them returned to the suite.

Ilia laid out the plan for Sergei Kuzmich to the team. "Sergei is known to be a night owl, enjoying the company of women. Sasha, Katherine and I will go to the downstairs bar in two hours. Zyra and Nick will stay in the room. Zyra will translate for Katherine. Sergei is treacherous. Do not believe anything he says. First, I have business to conduct from the boat. Two hours," he said as he left.

Sasha and Zyra went to their bedroom, Nick and Kiki to their own.

"Shall we make use of this fine bed?" asked Kiki. Her eyes twinkled. She hadn't poured all of her vodka out. Nick watched her turn down the bed, run her hand over the satin sheets. Nick's arms enveloped her from behind, and she leaned her head back against his chest to meet his lips. She reached around behind to grasp him, felt him stir, heard him gasp. Within his arms, she turned. Their kiss became more intense as he slid his hands up under her skirt. It was her turn to gasp. The danger they were facing intensified their lovemaking.

***

"Will Nick and Kiki be able to handle this mission?" Sasha asked Zyra.

Zyra reached over and traced a line down Sasha's chest, circling her breasts and moving downward. She loved the contrast of Sasha's pure white skin and her black fingers. "Nick and Katherine will be fine, but you must be the speaker. Kuzmich will be attracted to a strong woman. We want the vaccine, but he will lie. He cannot be trusted, but his greed is what will hold him to any deal."

Sasha moved under Zyra's fingers. "It has been too long since I felt your touch." She pulled Zyra's lips to hers, tongue exploring Zyra's mouth. Her own fingers began exploring Zyra's body.

Kiki fitted the earpiece under her hair, hiding it from sight. Zyra would translate the conversation for her while Sasha spoke to Kuzmich. "Testing 1 2 3," said Zyra. Kiki gave her thumbs up.

"Our crew is special forces. They will back us up," said Zyra, "and I will be listening. Any problems I will be there instantly."

Chapter Forty

October 4
Sochi, Russia

The bar was nearly empty. Heads turned as Sasha, Kiki and Ilia entered. Sasha spotted Sergei sitting alone at a table, his eyes glued to Kiki as they walked toward him.

"Sergei Kuzmich, I am Sasha Belikova," she said, holding out her hand. "I would like to introduce Ilia Belikov and Katherine Russell."

He stood, taking Kiki's hand and lifting it to his lips. "Charmed," he said in Russian. He turned to Ilia, holding out his hand. They shook as he gestured to the table. Again, his eyes rested on Kiki.

"Ms. Russell does not speak Russian," she said. If Kuzmich had noticed that Sasha and Ilia had the same last name, he didn't indicate it.

Sergei nodded. "Are you here on pleasure or business?" His eyes were still on Katherine.

The translation from Zyra came through clearly. Kiki showed no understanding of the conversation. "Business, but some pleasure, I think," said Sasha. "We came to meet with Major Verenich. Is he available?"

He turned to her with an intense look. "Unfortunately, he is away for an extended time. May I be of service?" His smile like a snake about to strike.

Sasha's eyebrows rose. "I'm not sure. We wish to buy product from Koltsovo."

Sergei frowned. "Alas, the last shipment of that particular product left port recently. We will not have more for two weeks. We already have a buyer."

"We will pay more," said Sasha. Behind Sergei's eyes, she knew the wheels were turning. She must be very careful with this Russian.

His eyes narrowed. "How much do you wish to buy?"

"We would make a deal for all of your product from Koltsovo."

Sergei's dark eyes flickered. "My customer pays well and would be most upset if they did not receive the product. Perhaps you could take part of the shipment."

"We pay better, much better," she repeated, watching the greed grow.

"I have concerns in any other deal. My protection is for the customer I have."

"We will double what your customer pays."

Sergei's lips were a tight line. "I can do that. Give me your number. I will call you one week before the shipment is to arrive here. I want half the money first."

Sasha laughed. "I think not, Sergei Kuzmich. I will give you ten percent now." She took off one earring and handed it to Kuzmich. "This is worth more than ten percent. I will expect it back when I pay you in full. It is part of a set." Sasha smiled.

He held it up to the light. The diamond flashed hypnotically. Kuzmich looked at her. "I will call you tomorrow with the schedule. I must go now. I have other business." He rose, bowed to Kiki, nodded to Ilia and left.

Kiki put her hand to her ear. Something was happening. She handed the earpiece to Sasha.

***

Nick rose to answer the knock at the door. Through the peephole, he saw a maid outside. As he unlocked the door, it burst open, knocking him back. The barrel of a Makarov was shoved in his face as two other men rushed in. With hands raised, he watched Zyra reach for a pistol. A crashing blow drove her to the floor.

"Who are you?" Nick cried. "What do want?"

A solid punch knocked the air out of him. He lay on the floor gasping. A voice like gravel rolling down a washboard barked in Russian. The third man went from room to room checking for others. The second man kept his gun pressed against Zyra's temple, pinning her head to the floor.

"What do you want with us?" asked Zyra in Russian.

"You are coming with us," grunted the man. "Now get up." He handed her a towel. "Wipe the blood from your face."

"We're not going anywhere," said Zyra, rising from the floor.

"You will come with us either by walking or in a laundry cart." He held up a syringe. "My boss wants to talk with you. Now move."

Ilia, Sasha and Kiki raced from the restaurant back to the hotel. Their suite was empty, signs of a struggle apparent. "They're gone!" wailed Kiki, "Nick's gone. Who could have taken them?"

"Sergei," said Ilia. "While we were dealing with him, his men took them."

Sasha was white with fury. "I will skewer that bastard," she snarled.

"I know this gang, and I know where they've gone, but first we go to the ship," said Ilia.

Chapter Forty-One

October 4
Sochi, Russia

Ilia faced the black-clad Special Forces team in the briefing room. Kiki and Sasha watched. "This gang has a warehouse near here that they use as their headquarters for their smuggling operations. It is isolated this time of night and has easy access to the water. They are holding Nick and Zyra there." On a monitor, his pointer highlighted a building on a map of the port. "It is a place of many uses for this gang." A plan of the building appeared. "Three points of egress." He pointed, "One, two, three. We will hit them simultaneously. Take out the guards, taser Sergei. We want to question him. Let's move!"

"Why did you kill Major Verenich?" Sergei Kuzmich shouted at Zyra, stripped and bound to a chair. The overhead lamp spotlighted her, the only light pushing back the darkness. Her head was up, staring into Kuzmich's eyes, her mouth a tight line. His hand lashed out with a loud crack that echoed around the warehouse. Blood flowed from her nose and down her face.

"You did me a big favor. I was planning to get rid of the major, but you did it for me. Why?" He pulled a knife from his belt and ran the point across her cheek.

Zyra remained silent as a thin rivulet of blood dripped from her jaw.

Sergei stepped back. "It does not matter. I spoke with the rest of your party. But you know that. They want to buy product from Koltsovo that is already sold. Ha!" He held up the earring. "She gave me this to secure the deal. I will have the other and the American woman."

Zyra's eyes followed the earring.

"I leave for Koltsovo tonight and will take the American with me." Sergei nodded at Nick then looked back at her, his eyes dead. "Somebody will pay for him. I think not for you, so unfortunately, you will not be going." He turned toward the three captors. "Take the

American to the car. Kill her." He pulled on his long black leather coat, turning away.

Simultaneously, three doors blew in, knocking Sergei to the ground. Men flooded the room, firing suppressed submachine guns. The three guards went down to the low pop pop pop. Sergei rose on his elbows as a dart struck his side. He jerked as the electric charge immobilized him.

Kiki ran to Nick. "Are you alright? Did they hurt you?"

"No. I'm okay."

Kiki cut his hands free.

Sasha rushed to untie Zyra, giving her a hug as she stood. "Thank God you're alive. I was sick with fear."

"I am fine." She hugged Sasha back, then strode over to the paralyzed Sergei. Rolling him over, she stood, looking into his eyes. Zyra knelt, removed his coat and stood, putting it on. Reaching down, she took his knife from his belt. She held it up. The tip still had a smear of her blood. Her hand a blur, she grabbed his hair and pulled his head back. With a single motion, slit his throat from ear to ear. Everybody froze, mouths agape. Zyra stepped back so the fountain of blood wouldn't soil her new coat.

"Why did you do that?" cried Ilia. "We needed to question him."

Zyra looked at Ilia. "We got our answers from Verenich. This piece of shit," she kicked the twitching body, "had nothing to add." She threw the knife into the spreading pool of blood as if it were something foul.

"How are we going to get our shipment?" asked Kiki.

"He wasn't going to sell it to you. He was going to rob you." She looked at Ilia. "We go to Koltsovo."

Chapter Forty-Two

October 5
White House, Washington, D.C.

"Mr. President, we had problems in Sochi," said Ron Carson, looking through the monitor at the president.

President Donaldson looked out the window of the Oval Office. Snags were inevitable. "Are we moving to Plan B?" he asked, looking at the members of his team.

"Our crew is making up Plan B as they go along, so yes, sir."

"What happened?"

"We were trying to set up a deal to buy the vaccine, but the dealer turned on us. He was killed."

"What's next?"

"Our team will go to Koltsovo to deal directly with the laboratory."

"Mr. President," said Sharon Volgyi, "The fact that the dealer wouldn't accept a higher money offer tells us he was locked into the arrangement with the Chinese. Either they had already paid him, or his protection was tied to them. My bet is both. That implicates someone in the Russian government as collaborating with China. How high up, we don't know."

"I want to find out," said the president. "Forward those instructions to our team. Get the vaccine. Find out who's behind the Chinese buy."

"Yes, Mr. President," said Ron, wondering if his team was up to it and how they'd accomplish it.

October 5
Sochi, Russia

On board the boat, Ilia, Kiki, Nick, Zyra, Sasha, and Lieutenant Mendez were gathered in the briefing room. Ron Carson and David Kennedy had just finished relaying the president's instructions to them via the secure link.

"Any ideas how to handle this?" he asked. "I know this is short notice, but I'd like to hear some brainstorming."

Ilia looked at the others. "Secretary Carson, the logistics of getting to Koltsovo and getting the shipment out are the problem. I suggest we go to Ukraine."

"Please call me Ron, and Ukraine is the wrong direction, if my geography is right."

"It is, and it isn't. I propose we go there and charter an Anotov AN 124. From Odeso, we fly to Novosibirsk. There I have trucks to drive to the Vector Institute. Once we get the shipment, we return to the plane and fly trucks and cargo to Anchorage, Alaska. The Anatov has the lift capacity and range to do this. Most importantly, it is a Russian aircraft. We can come up with a flight plan and fake clearances." He shrugged, awaiting comment on his plan.

"You just came up with that plan in five minutes?"

Ilia smiled. "Agents in the field must have contingencies."

"Yes, I'm sure they do. Where do you see the problems?"

Ilia nodded, appreciative that Ron thought to ask. "We must accomplish several tasks on short notice. The first is to charter the plane. The

Company has done that in the past. It comes with a complete crew. The pilots may not go along with what we want, so we must be prepared with our own Russian-speaking pilot qualified on the AN 124. With a barrel of money, we can convince the crew. We will be disguised as a secret Russian unit. We will need Russian uniforms for the SEAL team along with weapons." He grinned. "I can supply those. The trucks will have Russian military markings. They will be refrigerated and need to operate at times during the flight to keep the cargo chilled. We will need clearances with no questions asked in Alaska." One eyebrow rose. "It wouldn't do to get shot down by our own Air Force. We'll need a bundle of rubles to pay off anyone who needs it."

David Kennedy spoke up through the monitor. "You've given me quite a to-do list. I'll get on it. Anything else?"

Ilia looked at the group.

Nick spoke up. "We'll need to interrogate people."

"Right," said Ron. "We'll arrange for your equipment to be crated and moved onto the plane in Odeso."

"We'll need additional sound suppression and vibration isolation equipment because of the plane," said Nick. "A crate that's a sound chamber would be best."

"I'll get on it," said Ron. "Anything else?"

"It will take us several days to sail to Odeso, time to get things going. We'll be back to you tomorrow," said Ilia. The connection was broken.

There was silence in the room. They were about to embark on an incredibly dangerous mission. The peril was not lost on them.

Chapter Forty-Three

October 8
Casa Grande, Arizona

Stephen Sabino and Sheriff Brad Tierman looked at the lights of the city below. A month ago, the sight would not have been special. Tonight it was remarkable. Power was restored to the city after a month of outages. The automatic controls for the electric network were now manual and isolated from the commercial grid control systems. The Gila Bend power plant was up and running. To the north, the glow of lights from Phoenix was absent.

"We'll never be back to what things were before September 11," said Stephen, "but we've come a long way since then." He clapped the sheriff on the back. "Great job."

"Thanks, but it wasn't me who did it. It was all of us. We've learned the meaning of community again. The problem we're facing is refugees. We've done a fair job with those trickling in from California. The desert expanse between here and there keeps that flow small. Phoenix is another problem altogether. Power is slowly being restored, but large parts of the cities burned due to fires started during the riots. Rioters got shot. Glad I'm not there. The only bright spot for them is no smallpox."

"What about Tucson? Are we getting refugees from there?"

Brad sighed. "Not many. Tucson is almost back on track. They've managed to restore power by using the local gas turbine generator plants and keeping them off-grid. Smallpox hasn't shown up yet either, probably due to the new attitude."

He shook his head and looked down. "They've quarantined themselves, keeping out anybody who may be infected. It's a fortress city mentality, and we're seeing more of that. Unlike us, they don't have the resources to self-sustain and need to bring in food from Mexico. We will send surplus food to them when our crops come in, but if refugees keep coming here from Phoenix, we won't have any surplus. Our resources will be stretched thin, and we may have to take on the new mentality, as well."

"It hasn't even been thirty days since this attack. Look how far we've come," said Stephen.

"Yeah, we've come a long way, but we're getting reports that the big cities and much of the east coast is collapsing. The electric grid in the east is still down and may be for months. The logistics to support the high population centers is falling apart. People in America are literally starving to death. Smallpox is devastating the large cities, and shoot-to-kill orders have been issued to troops enforcing quarantines. There are open gun battles between troops and bands of refugees trying to flee down the I-95 corridor ahead of winter. America is tearing itself apart."

"Brad, Stephen," Miriam called from the house. "Nick's on the phone. He wants to talk to you."

"Coming, Mom," said Stephen.

"Hey, guys," came Nick's voice through the speakerphone. "Mom and Barb filled me in a little on how things are going. Lights are back on in the city."

"Yeah," said Brad, as he and Stephen joined Miriam and Barbara at the table. "We're dealing with refugees coming from Phoenix and Gila Bend, but so far we're coping."

"Refugees!" exclaimed Kiki, amazement in her voice.

"It's those poor people from the cities," said Miriam, her voice quavering. "They left everything behind. Lord, the stories they're telling," she whispered.

Barbara put out a hand to reassure Miriam. "We're volunteer-teaching. The kids don't hold back with their accounts."

"We've been getting some pretty bad reports on the large cities and the east coast," said Brad. "The power grids are still out in many areas. Couple that with the quarantine enforced by Army and Marine troops, and it's an ugly picture. Without power, they have no water. Drinking water is trucked in. Large parts of the cities have burned. No water for sanitation, the sewers don't work. In addition to smallpox, they're seeing typhoid now."

"You can't blame people for wanting to get out," cried Miriam. "People are getting shot by our own troops."

"That has happened in some cities," confirmed Brad. "Marshall Law has been declared. People are required to stay home, indoors to minimize any spread of disease. Enforcement of that keeps people from gathering to demonstrate. Peaceful demonstrators turned violent as frustration built at the inability of the government to protect and provide for them.

Yeah, people got shot. Now there are impromptu militias forming and sniping at troops. It's a war zone. We're fighting ourselves and losing."

There was no sound from Nick or Kiki.

"But not in Casa Grande," added Stephen. "Nick, what can you tell us about where you are or what you're doing?"

Not a very subtle change of subject, thought Kiki. Stephen didn't want to worry them. "We can't say much," she said. "Just know that we're part of a team trying to make this right."

She watched Nick. His head was down, shoulders slumped. She felt the helplessness, too, but it was Nick's family. "We may not be able to contact you for a while," Kiki said.

"Take care of each other," Nick added in a soft voice. "We have to go now."

The hiss of empty airwaves came from the speaker. Kiki reached over, turned it off. "They'll be okay." She wasn't as sure as she sounded. She put an arm around Nick.

Chapter Forty-Four

October 9
Situation Room,
Camp David, Maryland

"It was necessary, Mr. President," said Secretary of State, Sharon Volgyi. "You could not concentrate on the crisis facing the country if danger lurked outside your door or intruded into your mind."

"I ran from the crisis by leaving Washington." He sighed, giving a wry smile. "Let's get on with this meeting." He looked at the large monitor mounted on the wall. "Doctor Albertson, what's the status of the Center for Disease Control and the plague?"

"The good news is that we've received and distributed the vaccine shipment."

"How did you distribute it?" asked the president. "I'm not looking to criticize, I need to know."

"Mr. President, we had to triage the distribution. There were hard decisions to be made."

The president let him talk. Though he wanted the answer, he didn't want to think what triage meant. But Albertson needed to unload his conscience.

"Primary recipients of the vaccine were law enforcement, health workers, and the troops. Next, we focused on the areas outside of the quarantine sites. We ran out before that effort was finished."

The president closed his eyes. "So, those in the quarantine zones are condemned."

"Mr. President, the system is overwhelmed. People are working sixteen-hour days. We're going to lose some of them if we keep up this pace. We're trying to make those within the quarantine zone as comfortable as possible."

The president held up a hand. "It wasn't a criticism, Joel. I know you and your people are flat out. It's something I must know. What's the fatality rate?"

"We are seeing 40,000 deaths a day," Albertson said in a low voice. "Those are the reported ones. We estimate the actual number is twice that." Albertson's eyes were red, tears leaking from them.

"Thank you, Joel." The monitor with his face went black. "Where are we with the North Korean cyber attack?" He looked at George Pickering,

"We've been able to block any further hacks from them. We've designed an attack of our own and have a way into their system. David will tell you about that."

David Kennedy cleared his throat. "We have an agent in the tech center who will give us a window. We're awaiting your go ahead."

The president looked at General Edwards. "Tom, what are your thoughts on a strike?"

"Mr. President, it must be a crippling strike. A hack is not enough. They can rebuild within months. If we take out their trained technicians...."

"This is a military strike you're talking about?" asked the president.

"I am, sir. We could use cruise missiles and level the tech center."

"Isn't it next to a hospital?"

"Yes, sir."

"How hard would we need to hit it?"

"A lot of it is underground. We'd use bunker busters. The hospital would be destroyed."

"Alternatives?" asked the president, looking around the table.

"The only other thing I see is a boots on the ground raid," said David Kennedy.

"Okay, let's set that aside for now. Ron, where are we on the vaccine mission?"

"The boat with our team docked in Odeso last night. Tomorrow night after everything is loaded, they will leave for Novosibirsk. Our agent," he nodded at CIA Director Kennedy, "is making arrangements for permits and transportation. We hope to be in Koltsovo the following day."

"Any word from the shipping company regarding the hijackers' twenty million dollar ransom for the ship?"

"They came back with a ten million dollar offer. I think they're stalling while the search intensifies."

"Mr. President," said Sharon Volgyi, "the stalling is telling us that whatever their plans, time is not tight. My sources tell me the European Union has made a deal with China to open their markets fully to Chinese goods. In return, China has promised to get Russia to pull its forces back."

"How the hell are they going to do that?" Something nefarious, thought the president. "China and Russia are only on good terms because China is buying Russian oil and gas. Are they going to threaten to cut back? Will that work?"

"There is a glut of oil in the world now because the U.S. imports have tanked," said Volgyi. "China's threat to cut back on purchases may not be enough to convince President Vladimirov to pull back. He has coveted the eastern European nations that were once part of the USSR. The cutback is a long-term issue. He may opt to strike quickly, dealing with the economic fallout later."

"What's the status of the Russian forces arrayed along their western border?"

"They pulled troops from everywhere to create a 300,000 strong force," said General Edwards. "Logistics are not fully in place yet. When they are, Russia could pull the trigger at any time."

"How long until that point?" asked the president.

"Estimates are no sooner than ten days. The attack could come anytime after that. We've informed NATO and our European allies, who are moving troops to the eastern borders now."

"What can we do to discourage this attack?" asked the president.

"We can deploy Air Force units to Germany and Turkey to support troops at the southern end of the border. We can also move USS George Bush battle group near the coast of Latvia. Germany, Finland and Norway will give us support," said General Edwards.

"We can't give any ground support?" asked the president.

"Sir, we stripped our units to maintenance levels only, bringing the troops back to the U.S." He looked steadily at the president. "We have no one to send."

"With the quarantine of the United States, I'm not sure they would be accepted," said Secretary of State Volgyi.

Europe will have to pull their own chestnuts out of the fire, thought the president.

Chapter Forty-Five

October 11
Novosibirsk Airport, Russia

Kiki felt like crap. Something had her system upset. If she weren't in the bathroom, giving up last night's dinner, she was purging yesterday's meals. Sometimes she was doing both at the same time. She ached all over. The SEAL medic said it was something she ate. Nick agreed and put her to bed on a makeshift cot in the front of the plane. The chill in her mind was familiar. She froze.

"Not well are we, Katherine?"

Oh God! Not now. "I'm feeling like warmed-over shit," she yelled in her mind.

"I can sense your distress. With everything going on in the world, there is so much hatred and fear I am dining well."

"I can't say I'm happy for you. Go away. I don't feel up to dealing with you now."

"I want to give you information. The Russian President hates the west with an intense passion I find quite tasty. He has spoken of plans to regain lost parts of the USSR. He says doing so will destroy the influence of the United States."

"Well, that's not news," sneered Kiki.

"In itself it is not. There are large concentrations of troops along the western border. Some are frightened, but it is not the sharp tang of normal battle fear. This has a sickly taste I do not care for."

A large concentration of troops, thought Kiki. Was Russia preparing to invade Eastern Europe? What would a sickly taste mean? "Are they afraid of dying?"

"There is that, but this is a different fear, like a tang of guilt. Some have spoken of doing something wrong."

Were they considering using tactical nuclear weapons? She needed to pass this information on to Nick. Kiki tried to rise. Another bout of nausea struck. She reached for the bucket next to her bed.

"Ta ta, Katherine. I will be back."

Nick appeared, pushing the makeshift curtain aside. "How are you doing?"

Kiki pulled her head from the bucket and looked at him.

"Okay, command decision here," said Nick. "You're staying."

Kiki tried to shake her head no, but a wave of nausea stopped her.

"Ilia went to Koltsovo as soon as we landed in Novosibirsk. He has contacts so by the time we get there everything should be set. We're leaving in ten minutes and should be back in a few hours." He leaned down and kissed the top of her head. "Get better, love."

"Be careful," she whispered. Kiki knew she'd be a liability to the mission in her present state. Nick made the right decision.

The sixty-kilometer drive to the Vector Institute was eerily quiet. Little traffic was on the road. They saw no military anywhere. Nick tried to doze, catch any sleep he could, but Russia intruded into his thoughts. He became alert as the truck stopped at a manned gate. It was hours before dawn and the sleepy guard came out of the warm shack to approach the driver's door.

Nick watched Sergeant Gagarin lean out and hand him the false papers. The guard looked at them, handed them back. He returned to the shack, pushed a button, and the gate creaked open.

Through their headsets, Ilia directed them to the production laboratory building. Grabbing the small duffle bag, Nick and the sergeant walked through the steel door, leaving the team with the two trucks. Ilia met them inside. He looked at the bag and nodded.

"We have two agents here. They are not aware of each other. Dr. Malikov is our primary contact." Ilia led them through a door where a pudgy middle-aged man stood as they entered. He smiled through a pockmarked face, extending a hand. Nick shook it. Mailkov's eyes darted to the bag. Ilia said something in Russian. Malikov nodded.

As they walked down the deserted hall, Ilia whispered to Nick, "I told him the money would be his when the shipments are loaded on the trucks." Nick nodded.

At the loading dock area were eight pallets with white plastic drums secured to them. Each pallet had four drums with Cyrillic markings. Why did they need two trucks? Nick wondered. These eight pallets would easily fit in a single truck. Ilia spoke to the team, and they heard the truck engines start. Within a minute, Ilia opened the rollup door where the two trucks had backed against the dock.

Sergeant Gagarin started a fork lift, studied the controls for a second and proceeded to load the four pallets on one truck. He then loaded another box sitting near the pallets. Ilia walked to a second set of pallets. These also had drums strapped to them. The marking were different. As he watched, Ilia pulled out a rag, doused it with liquid and wiped away the markings. He pulled labels from his pocket and attached them to the drums. As soon as he was done, Sergeant Gagarin loaded them on the second truck.

Ilia nodded to Nick who handed the bag to the eager Dr. Malikov, who climbed into the cab of the first truck. "He goes with us. That was the deal I had to make. The investigation will lead to him. He has to be gone. The sergeant will take good care of you."

"Aren't you coming with us?" asked the Nick, worry in his voice.

"I'm going with the other truck."

"I'll see you at the airport, though, right?" Nick wasn't sure what was happening.

"I'm taking another route. I have one more mission before I retire from Russia. See you in the U.S." He clapped the dazed Nick on the shoulder. "The box contains your next assignment. Pump him dry." Ilia laughed as he lowered the roll-up door and climbed into the truck cab. As the sun was coming up, they roared through the gate and onto the highway.

At the Novosibirsk airport, Nick's truck drove through the commercial gate and straight into the AN 124. The ramp closed behind them as the engines started. The AN 124 crew and the SEAL team secured the truck to the deck, and they headed for their seats to belt in. Nick had barely strapped into his harness before the acceleration pulled at him to the roar of the huge turbofan engines.

Major Pushkin watched the giant AN 124 take off. Meaninglessly, he screamed for it to stop. In utter frustration, he fired his pistol at the departing plane until the magazine was empty.

First, the gate guard notified him of two transport trucks entering the Vector Institute at an odd schedule. Their papers seemed to be in order, but Pushkin had no notice of a shipment scheduled for departure. His calls to Colonel Noskov went unanswered, as did his calls to Dr. Malikov. He got to the production building in time to see the two trucks departing. Racing to the carpool for his car, he followed. When one truck took the airport turnoff, he had to decide which to follow. He went to the airport. He would contact Colonel Noskov to set up roadblocks for the other truck.

By the time he got through the commercial freight security, the huge plane was taking off. Something was wrong. His search for Noskov and Malikov was fruitless. At the control tower he was told the flight was a Special Forces charter for cargo destined for Novogorod. He knew of the troop movements to the west, but would they need biological agents? The first tremors of fear sprang up in his mind. Who were these people and what had they taken? He had to get back to the Institute. He had to talk to Colonel Noskov.

Chapter Forty-Six

October 11
Camp David, Maryland

"Mr. President, our shipment is in the air," announced CIA Director David Kennedy. "They report no problems and a strange absence of military traffic."

"Vladimirov has pulled all available military and moved them to the western borders," said General Edwards. "Mr. President, the whole eastern side of Russia is defenseless. An opportunity for China." There was silence as those present digested this news.

"Are we seeing a buildup of Chinese troops along the border?" asked the president, looking at his crisis team.

"The Chinese raised the alert level along their border. They are moving troops that way, but not in numbers we expect for an all-out invasion."

"They would be unopposed," noted Sharon Volgyi.

"True. They could drive all the way to the oil and gas fields, but it would take a lot more troops to hold that territory," said Edwards.

"Maybe holding it is not their intent," countered Volgyi. "Under the label of exercises, they are also deploying troops toward the Pacific coast. It's slow." She frowned. "We're having trouble confirming this. What we can say is that this represents a lot of troop movement and activity. The objective is not clear."

The president started to speak, then stopped. "Could this have anything to do with the purchase of smallpox vaccine?"

"Who were they intending to vaccinate?" asked Sharon Volgyi. "If the shipping company becomes more anxious to get the shipment back, the timetable may be moving up."

"Their search efforts intensified, satellite and air coverage has grown. Internet activity is ramping up," added George Pickering.

"We're good," said Ron Carson. "The ship doesn't look the same. The registry is Spanish."

"What about the crew?" asked the president.

"They're being held onboard, completely isolated."

"Tom, how long until our Air Force and Navy forces are in position to aid NATO if the Russians invade?"

"Forces will be in place within two days, sir. Logistics and support are following as quickly as we can move. Sir...."

"Go ahead, Tom. Give us the downside."

"Our forces will be at huge risk from land-based and submarine attacks. We are in Ivan's waters, his backyard. In the event of war, we face losses, perhaps major. Russian naval forces are already moving in to northern waters. I've brought in an additional naval task force. I'm moving the Carl Vinson carrier battle group closer to Turkey on the southern side."

The president nodded approval. "Before we commit more forces to the European operation, let's see what China's doing. We must protect homeland America." Those around the table nodded agreement.

"What about our domestic situation? Dr. Albertson, where is our own manufacture of vaccine?"

"The first production is starting to trickle out. Within thirty days, we'll be in full production."

The president allowed a small smile. "What about the inoculation process? How long will that take to gear up and get those units in the field?"

"Our plan is to flood the streets with thousands of mobile stations. We are poised to begin this program within two days of the arrival of the vaccine from Russia."

"How many inoculations are coming?" asked Ron Carson.

Dr. Albertson ran a hand through his wispy hair. "We used twenty milliliters as the inoculation dose from the last shipment. We are assuming this shipment is of the same strength. Each drum will yield ten million inoculations. That's the math, sir. In reality, there will be losses and spoilage. Conservatively, we can expect to inoculate five million people from each drum. The reports of thirty-two in the shipment will allow us to inoculate ninety million people."

Smiles appeared around the table. This was good news. The president tapped on his tablet for a few minutes. "By my reckoning, if you had 5000 stations, it would take you twenty days to use up the shipment, inoculating twenty-four hours a day."

"That may be a bit optimistic, sir. We figured thirty," said Dr. Albertson.

"Ladies and gentlemen, that's too long. In that thirty days we will lose an additional one million people."

"More than that, sir," said Dr. Albertson. "Even with emergency inoculations, we are going to lose most of those people in quarantine. Thirty million people are quarantined at present."

"Thirty million," gasped the president. "Thirty million," he repeated in a whisper. "Dr. Albertson, I want emergency training of National Guard and military personnel to give inoculations. I want twenty thousand stations working around the clock."

"We can do that, sir, but we'll run out of vaccine in ten days. We're studying the disease transmission vectors now. If we could cut those vectors down, the spread of the disease could be slowed."

"Joel, you know how best to attack this. Let me know what we can do to help." The mood was somber again. "Ron, what's happening with restoring the electrical grid?"

"Mr. President, we have everything running we had parts for. We can do no more until we get replacement parts. Many of the small communities are up to normal because they had smaller generation plants and took their system off-grid. They are operating manually. Large swaths of the east coast and west coast are still dark. We moved portable generator plants into critical areas and manually set them up. One of the problems is manpower."

"Manpower!" exclaimed the president. "Surely, there are thousands of operators to help with this."

"There are, sir, but most of them never saw manual switchgear, and fewer of them have done hands-on work with high voltage. We're working to correct that. The problem we will have in the northeast is that winter is coming. We're going to open shelters in every school. We must get the water system working again to get the sewer system operating. A shelter is no good without operating bathrooms."

"What about food and water?" asked Sharon Volgyi.

"We're giving our farmers whatever they need to produce food. We've also opened the borders to imports from Mexico. One problem is that the value of the dollar has plummeted. The peso and the dollar are equal. Mexico is asking us to keep refugees from fleeing across the border into Mexico. We don't have the manpower. In Juarez and Tijuana, Mexican soldiers are shooting crossers. They're using flamethrowers on the bodies."

Chapter Forty-Seven

October 12
Over Siberia

Nick was in the sound box preparing the isolation chamber. The vibration of the plane came through his feet, but there was little sound. The long box that was loaded along with the vaccine contained Colonel Noskov. He had information they needed.

He and Zyra laid the unconscious colonel in the chamber and Nick attached the IVs and the monitor pads. With his laptop, Nick checked to ensure the sensors were working. Zyra sat beside him as he began to wake up Noskov. Kiki was with them, but obviously still not feeling well.

Noskov's heart rate increased along with respiration and brainwave. The colonel was waking up into a lightless soundless existence.

"Where am I?" Zyra translated. They said nothing. "What is this place?" They said nothing.

Nick needed to find where Noskov's mind would go when confronted with an environment of nothing. His body gave him no sensory input. When his existence was only his consciousness, where would his mind go? Nick triggered the mic and breathed into it.

"Who is there?" asked the colonel.

Nick breathed again.

"Who is that? Where am I?"

"Oh, Victor, is that you?"

"Who are you?" Noskov screamed.

"Victor, my sweet baby. You don't know me?" cooed Zyra.

"Mama, is that you?"

"Who else, Victor?"

"But Mama, you're dead."

"Yes, I am."

"Mama, I tried to help you and Papa, but I couldn't. I tried to take care of Mikhail, but he wanted to be a soldier."

"Mikhail wanted to be like you. He always wanted to be like his big brother."

"I know, Mama. When we got to Afghanistan, I put him in a desk job, nice and safe, but he wouldn't stay. He disobeyed my orders and went out with the helicopter forces. It was the Mujahidin who killed him when they shot his helicopter down using American missiles. It was because of the Americans he died. But we are going to make them pay."

"How can you make them pay? America is so strong, they are so many."

"We have made an alliance with another great enemy of America. We have begun our attack on their homeland. While they struggle to recover, they have left our former provinces without their NATO protection. They have pulled their soldiers back to the United States. Without them, NATO is weak. We will take back what is ours. The Union of Soviet Socialist Republic will rise again."

"But Victor, so many more of our young men will die."

"But Mama, we'll be a world power again. We'll command respect."

"America will grow strong. They will attack us."

"No Mama, our allies will invade America while we take back Eastern Europe. America will no longer be a threat to us. Mama, is Mikhail with you?"

"Yes, Victor, he is with us."

Nick increased the sedatives, putting Noskov to sleep. He turned to Zyra. "We have to get this information back as soon as possible. This is stunning news." Zyra nodded.

The pilot of the AN 124 looked at the fuel gauge again. He tapped it to see if it was stuck. It didn't budge. Uh oh. He called back to the lieutenant on the intercom. "I need to see you in the cockpit."

Chapter Forty-Eight

October 12
Camp David, Maryland

The door to the Oval Office burst open. "Mr. President," exclaimed Ron Carson, "we've just received word the team won't be able to reach Anchorage."

"Gentlemen, please excuse us," said the president, signaling the end of the meeting. The men filed out. The guard closed the door.

"What happened, Ron?" asked President Donaldson.

"A malfunction with the plane, sir. They are looking for an emergency landing site now. We're scrambling a C-17. We'll divert it to the AN-124 wherever it has to put down."

"Inside Russia! What about their defenses? We can't just fly a C-17 into Russian airspace."

"No sir, General Edwards is working out a way in. We've also received a transcript of the interrogation of Colonel Noskov." Ron handed the transcript to the President. "Nick Sabino conducted the session with the help of an interpreter. The highlighted parts," Ron pointed at the document, "are the relevant parts."

The president scanned through the file, his face growing pale as he read. "An invasion! Who?"

"It all points to the Chinese. They are moving troops into the port cities. They bought both smallpox virus and vaccine. The plague came from them. They hired the Russian gang to distribute it. They mean to invade, sir."

The president sat very still for a moment. "I'm not so sure. Get General Edwards on the line." The president sat back for a few minutes while the connection was made. "Tom, what happened?"

"Sir, they have a fuel leak and can't make Anchorage. We're directing them to a small strip, Sberbank, near the town of Marcovo. They will land there. We'll put the C-17 down next to them. They're loading everything into the semi holding the vaccine. We'll drive the semi onto the C-17 and be off with them. Shouldn't take more than fifteen minutes."

"And the Russian defenses?" asked the president.

"Sir, I've scrambled the 356th Air Wing from Japan. We're bringing in four F-35s and a Super Wild Weasel team. They'll rendezvous just outside of Russian airspace. With your approval, we'll proceed to the site."

"What's a Super Wild Weasel team?" asked Ron Carson.

"During the Viet Nam war, electronics detection and destruction planes would go in ahead of a mission," explained General Edwards. "They would get painted by enemy radar and hopefully launch a missile at that site before they got shot down. It was hairy work. Today we use a team consisting of two specially designed drones and a B-2 stealth bomber. They enter the theater in tight formation, looking like a large single plane. When the enemy launches antiaircraft missiles, the drones split off drawing the missiles away. The stealth bomber has such a small radar signature the missiles ignore it, but it carries a load of anti radar missiles. The drones are very fast, and able to outmaneuver the attacking missiles. Thirty-five G turns are no problem, something a pilot couldn't survive. They are the bait. The B-2 is the trap. We can punch through the Russian missile defenses."

Ron nodded.

"You have my permission," said the president.

"Our latest intelligence says all of the Russian military aircraft have been moved to the eastern border. What's left is the missile defense. They will light us up – we will respond. It's going to get messy on the ground. I've got an air tanker accompanying the C-17 to the Russian coast so our boys can get a drink. We should be able to rotate them so our team always has air cover."

"Tom, is this going to work?"

"Sir, without the Russian Air Force, we can knock out their missiles, minimizing any threat. We don't think they even have ground troops within striking range. There might be a few militia."

The president sighed deeply. "Russia's concentrated everything on the European border. Secretary Volgyi tells me that the Russian nationals in Latvia and Lithuania are protesting and forming resistance groups. It's the tried and true Russian formula, a repeat of Ukraine. Under the guise of protecting their citizens, they will invade. God help NATO and Europe. If they strike Russian forces within Russian borders, I wouldn't put it past Vladimirov to use tactical nukes. Then what?"

"General Edwards, How do you interpret China's buildup?" asked Ron Carson.

"Mr. President, Ron, I'm worried. Our naval forces are deployed, as are our air wings. We probably could not prevent an invasion, particularly with the size of the forces China is marshaling. Yet if we recall our forces, it leaves our allies at risk."

"I agree with you, Tom, but I don't see an invasion in the cards," said the president. "The logistics of supporting an invasion force, of holding territories they take are too great. They might take it, but they couldn't hold it. So why do it? Why the buildup of forces?"

"I understand what you're saying, Mr. President," said Ron. "Perhaps the buildup is to hold us back from full support of NATO. The bio-attack has forced our ground troops to stay here. Colonel Noskov said they had an alliance."

"But what's in it for China?" asked the president.

Chapter Forty-Nine

October 12
Marcovo, Russia

The huge Anatov AN-124 barely stopped rolling and Lieutenant Richard Mendez was on his feet. "Let's go people. Secure the perimeter. Get that vehicle on the ground." Four SEALs jumped to the ground as soon as the ramp was open. Two others got behind the semi to direct the driver. The flyover had revealed nothing but a few small aircraft and no sign of soldiers. The Russian Anatov airplane and the heavily armed guards should deter any inquiries from locals.

"Keep your people inside," the lieutenant said to Nick. "Our uniforms have no markings. Anybody looking will assume we're Russian. They won't bother us. By the time the C-17 is on the ground, it'll be too late to do anything. We'll be gone in a blink."

"What about the Russian Air Force?" asked Nick.

"According to our intel, they're gone, same for ground troops. We'll have a couple of F-35s orbiting overhead, just in case we missed something. The flyboys punched a hole in the missile defense to get here. They'll do the same when we leave."

"How long before they get here?" asked Kiki, peeking around the curtain.

"Feeling better?" asked Mendez.

"I'll live," said Kiki.

"Last update said F35s in thirty minutes, C-17 in about an hour."

"Lieutenant, come take a look," shouted a voice from outside. "We got company. What you want I should do?"

He turned to Sasha. "We may need an interpreter. There's a uniform hanging in the locker that should fit." He pointed and turned. "Katherine, the AR-10 is in the locker if we need to convince anyone to stay away. Don't kill anyone unless they need it." He turned toward the door.

From the cockpit, Katherine had a good view of the distant buildings. Eight-hundred yards away a group of figures walked across the grassy field. She focused the twelve power scope on the tallest one. By his gestures, it was obvious he was the leader. God! He looked old. She looked at one of the other soldiers. Kids, they were kids. These weren't soldiers. "Mendez," she said into the com unit, "it's just kids and old people. Must be a militia of some sort."

"Okay, Sasha and I will go meet them. Keep us covered. Kids or not, they have guns. If you let them shoot us, I'll hurt you." He laughed at the joke.

Kiki watched them walk toward the group. Sasha and Mendez saluted the old man. He returned the salute. Sasha began speaking as Mendez looked threatening. The old man pointed to the sky in the east. Sasha pointed behind the small force. They saluted and turned back.

"It was a local militia. They started practicing after the Army left. About an hour ago, they received an alert that foreign aircraft entered Russia. They're supposed to be on watch. I sent them back to guard the buildings and airplanes. I told them we'd inform command if anything shows up."

"Incoming!" shouted Mendez.

Everything shook as the two F-35s came in at near supersonic speed barely off the deck. One went straight up, wings waggling, the other stayed low and circled for another pass. Kiki watched the kids scatter for cover while the old man shouted at them. The US marking were easily visible.

Half an hour later, two more F-35s arrived with the C-17. They orbited while the plane touched down and taxied to them. Kiki looked for the old man. He was standing, rifle at this shoulder. Uh oh. She fired, striking the ground in front of him. She fired again, hitting to his right. The old man had enough. He scampered for the buildings, dropping the rifle. She policed her brass and ran for the big plane, engines idling.

The semi was loaded. SEALs were securing it as she found her web seat and strapped in. Seconds later, the engines roared, she was pushed into the straps. The vibration from the turboprops a welcome throb. The unwelcome but familiar tingling in her mind caused her to shudder.

"Nice job, Katherine. You terrified that old man. The fear was a tasty snack. See, you are still able to feed me. I do want to tell you that this little foray of your forces into Russia has raised fears of the leadership. The leader, Vladimirov, is holding it in check, telling himself it is nothing. If it is

something, it will create a banquet. Delicious times are coming for me. Not so much for you and Nick, I fear. Ta ta, Katherine."

God! Would this thing never leave her alone? The statement about the Russian president was interesting. Of course, he was informed about this incursion. From what they had seen, there was no defense of the motherland in the east. Russia was vulnerable.

Chapter Fifty

October 13
North America

The C-17 was on the ground at Elmendorf Air Force Base in Anchorage only long enough to refuel before departing for Seattle, where part of the vaccine was unloaded. On to San Francisco, where more vaccine was dropped off. At Los Angles, Nick and Kiki deplaned, along with the last of the vaccine.

"Zyra, Sasha, thank you for your help," said Nick. "We're ready for a break."

Zyra, face showing little expression said, "Thank you, Nick and Katherine. I continue to learn from you. Maybe someday I can interrogate suspects with your skill."

Sasha, not understanding, gave Zyra questioning look. "We return to Israel. Perhaps, we meet again." She shook Nick then Kiki's hands. The SEAL team waved from the plane as the ramp closed.

Zyra and Sasha nestled against each other in the webbing as the plane thundered down the runway.

"Two visits with Ilia in one month. Is that a record?" asked Zyra.

"We haven't been together much after our youth. Ilia wanted to return to Russia to work against the government after they killed our parents. I wanted to remain in Israel with our aunt."

"And good for me that you did," said Zyra, giving her arm a hug. "Are you worried about returning to Russia?"

"When we landed in Sochi, I had mixed feelings. It is the land of my birth, but the brutality common in that country led to the death of my parents." Sasha sighed, "I love Russia but hate those in charge. Our work in Koltsovo was satisfying. A small blow against those monsters. Anything we do against them I'm for."

"We're all working against them," said Zyra.

"Has he arrived in Haifa, yet?"

"I haven't heard. Perhaps Lieutenant Mendez knows." Zyra walked over to the lieutenant. "Have you any word of Ilia?"

"He will deliver his shipment to Haifa in two days. The Chinese ship departs after that. The captain wants to defect, by the way. He says he'll be executed for allowing his ship to be taken. Do you wish to help with the debriefing? You've done that work before."

"No, Lieutenant, I have only worked with Nick Sabino and Katherine Russell when questioning enemies. Their techniques would not be used on others."

"Yeah, I did notice that Colonel Noskov was still unconscious when he was carried off the plane in Los Angeles."

"If he's lucky, he'll never wake up," said Zyra in a low voice as she turned away.

The world in Haifa was untouched compared to where they'd been and what they'd seen. Arm-in-arm, Zyra and Sasha deplaned and headed for the Leonardo Hotel. They needed a night of soaking and bed. A bottle of fine red wouldn't hurt either.

Chapter Fifty-One

October 14
Camp David, Maryland

"Ladies and gentlemen, we have some good news along with the horrible news today," said the president. "Ron, fill us in on the Russian vaccine."

"Thank you, Mr. President. After a snag or two, the shipment of vaccine arrived on the west coast yesterday. Dr. Albertson will explain the distribution. Our interrogation of Colonel Noskov was enlightening. He claimed there was a conspiracy, and alliance to distribute the smallpox virus backed by a major world power." Ron looked at the faces attending the meeting.

"Yesterday, the Chinese shipping company paid the ransom for the ship and cargo. This was not the first purchase by this company of bio-agents from the Vector Institute in Koltsovo. We are returning the ship, but with another cargo. We suspect China may be the ally Noskov referred to. I'll let David Kennedy describe another troubling aspect."

The Director of the CIA looked up from his notes. "We know there has been a buildup of troops in the port cities of China. Our suspicion is that they are preparing to deploy, perhaps to our west coast. This is speculation, but we have no other answer for the troop movements. The bio-attack weakened us. Simultaneously, NATO is preparing for war with Russia in Eastern Europe. Our ground forces are deployed here because of the domestic disaster we face."

"To offer a differing opinion," said the president, "I'm not of the same mind about a Chinese invasion. It would be difficult if not impossible for them to keep what they take in any invasion. And as David said, our ground forces are here. We need to think more deeply on this. Ron, talk to your interrogators. See what's not in the report, what's not in the transcript. Perhaps Noskov has more to tell. Bring him back here for the experts." The president looked at the wall-mounted monitor. "Dr. Albertson, how is the battle against this pathogen going?"

"Mr. President, the shipment from Russia will save many lives. For the first time, we see a decline in the fatality rate."

"What is that rate, doctor?" asked the president.

"Last week, we peaked at 40,000 reported deaths per day. If yesterday is any indication, our average for next week will be 20,000. By the time the Russian vaccine is gone, our own production will be coming on line."

"That is good news," said the president, "though the image of 20,000 deaths per day tarnishes the gloss a bit."

"Yes, sir, it does," said Ron. "California was particularly hard hit by the virus and the loss of the electrical grid. It will require a massive investment to get it going again."

"And winter's coming in the northeast. Ron, where are we in restoring power to the east coast?"

"We're working as fast as we can, but the problem is parts. We are cranking up our domestic production of switchgear and transformers, but that is a slow process."

"So we could be facing a winter where the weather-related fatality rate exceeds that of the virus," said the president.

"We're working to prevent that, sir."

"The reality is," stated the president, "with the grid down, our fatality rate already exceeds that of the virus. When you consider food and water-related deaths, sanitation-related deaths, not to mention the increased death rate in hospitals because of the collapse of infrastructure, the sad fact, we may lose half our population. The United States will never be the same."

"Sir," said General Edwards, "those who did this to us must not go unpunished."

"Yes, Tom. But we must be subtle about it. Those behind this planned for a long time, planned for a world-changing set of events, and planned for the long term. We must do the same. We have to be equal to that task."

Chapter Fifty-Two

October 15
Casa Grande, Arizona

The blast of the departing helicopter whipped dust and leaves away from the driveway as Nick and Kiki turned toward the Sabino front door. The dry autumn air of Arizona was refreshingly pleasant, maybe more so because they were home. The front door burst open.

"God, it's good to see you." Stephen gushed. "How was the trip?"

"Long," said Kiki. "We left Alaska last night on a transport that hit every city between there and here."

"Alaska! What's in Alaska?"

"Not us, thank God!" said Kiki.

They laughed. "Mom and Barb are teaching at the refugee school. They should be home in a couple of hours. You guys want to relax by the pool and enjoy an adult beverage?"

"That sounds nice," said Nick. "I'll get the bags and put them in our room. Meet you there."

The large overhang kept their heads in shadow while their bodies were in the afternoon sun. The tension of the trip melted away as they settled into the deck chairs, the sun warming them, basking like lizards on a rock.

"To your return," said Stephen, returning with three beers. Nick and Kiki took theirs and raised them in agreement. "I suppose you can't say anything about what happened."

"We brought back vaccine," said Kiki, "a lot of vaccine. That's really all we can say for now."

In silence, they looked at the valley below. "The city's grown," remarked Nick. "How are things going here?"

"The population's increased by almost fifty percent. There are now six refugee camps outside the city limits." Stephen pointed at the large tent compounds. "In addition, many people within the city took in boarders. They get paid. It's been a strain on all of us."

The doorbell rang.

"I'll get it. You guys relax," Stephen said, rising.

"It sure feels good to be back here," sighed Nick. The peace and silence was profound.

"Yeah," agreed Kiki. She took a sip of her beer, looking from the valley to Nick. "I didn't say anything, but the Director visited me again on the flight back."

"Why didn't you tell me."

"It still creeps me out. I put it out of my mind. It did say things about fear within the Russian leaders, but I don't know what it means."

"Hey, travelers," Brad called, opening the sliding glass door. "I brought some people who say they need to see you." Brad stepped aside, letting Ron Carson and David Kennedy out onto the patio.

Nick and Kiki stood. "Lose the ties," said Nick, laughing. "You're in Arizona now."

"I'll get more IPAs." said Stephen, disappearing into the kitchen. "Brad, are you on duty?" He nodded.

"October in Arizona. This is nice," remarked Ron.

Stephen arrived with the beers and iced tea for Brad.

"Sheriff, you've done a good job with the city," complemented Ron, smiling at the sheriff.

"Reports I've gotten say you're becoming a model. How many refugees are housed here?"

"Fifteen thousand at the last count."

"They're in camps?" asked Kennedy.

"Most are in tent cities." Brad pointed into the valley. "Others are boarding with residents. We've put every able-bodied man woman and child to work at the farms. With the surplus of labor, what used to be done by tractor is done by hand."

"Kids too?" asked Ron.

"They work a farm shift and go to school on split shifts."

"Any trouble?" asked Carson.

Brad shrugged. "At first we had demonstrations. Petty theft climbed, too. Keeping everybody busy has made a difference. In the city, we have a continuous system of patrols by volunteers. We're coping."

"More than that, I'd say. I wasn't kidding about you being a model. We might have you consult," said Ron.

Brad smiled at the praise.

"Brad, Stephen, would you excuse us. We need to speak to Nick and Katherine," said David, smiling. As the door closed, the smile disappeared.

Ron placed his iPhone on the table. The voice of the president came through it. "Nick, Katherine, how are you? Recovering from your trip?"

"Good afternoon, Mr. President," said Kiki, a little stunned by his voice. "Yes, we're recovering, glad to be home. This visit by Secretary Carson and Director Kennedy is a surprise, as is your call."

"First, I want to thank you for a job well done. The information you sent us will be critical in guiding our actions toward those responsible for this heinous crime. I'm here with Director Pickering and General Edwards. We need to pick your brains a bit."

"How may we help you?" asked Kiki.

"Cut right to the chase, don't you, Katherine. I like that, so I will too. We've been trying to assess what's happening. The transcripts and tapes were great, but I want your feelings as you heard him talk. We're hoping there's more. Here's the short version of what we're seeing. China seems to be behind the bio-attack in the U.S. We don't have the smoking gun, but they bought bio-agents and vaccine. They are preparing troops for deployment, apparently for overseas. Some of my staff believe they intend to invade us. I am not convinced. So what are they up to? I want a free flow of thoughts and ideas. This is a brainstorming session. There are no embarrassing comments, okay. Nick, Kiki you've been in the thick of this, doing the interrogating and being in Russia. What do you see?"

Kiki sighed. "I agree that China is behind the bio-attack, hiring Russians to carry it out," she said. "I didn't get any idea that China might invade America. Did you, Nick? He's shaking his head no."

"An invasion is only good if you are able to hang on to what you take," exclaimed the president. "The other thing is that they have ruined the economy of their largest trading partner. Why would they do that? And what are they going to do about it? A billion hungry Chinese scares everyone. We have rumors of a Chinese-European Union deal to brunt the Russian attack in exchange for open markets."

"How would China do that?" asked Kiki, staring at Nick, neither understanding. Kiki felt a glimmer of an idea.

"Their bio-attack has diminished us, facilitating a Russian invasion of Eastern Europe," said Ron.

"What do they get in return?" posed the president.

"During the interrogation, we got the impression the Russian leadership was nervous about an attack on their eastern border," Kiki said. Nick started, puzzled. "Director Kennedy," she continued, "what response did you see to our rescue incursion?" Obviously, Nick wondered where this was coming from. Nothing like this came up in the questioning. Kiki winked and raised a finger, pointing up. Nick got it. They could say nothing about the Director.

"We picked up frantic messages," said George Pickering. "Several air wings were put on alert for possible redeployment against an attack by U.S. forces in Eastern Russia. When there was no follow-up by us, it reduced the threat level, but all missile defense batteries remain on full alert. They are acutely aware of their vulnerability with all their forces facing Europe."

"So, Mr. President, if there were a legitimate threat, Russia would have to redeploy forces to defend," said Kiki. She watched the light bulb go off in those around the table.

"There nothing to prevent China from invading and taking the oil and gas fields!" exclaimed Ron. "Two birds with one stone.

China deters the Russian invasion, opening up full trade with the EU under their agreement. They also get control of the oil and gas because Russia moved all their forces out of the way. Meanwhile, we are powerless in trying to maintain the status quo with our ground forces tied up domestically. Not that we'd interfere, anyway."

"I knew this call was a good idea," said the president. "You and Nick may not be geopolitical whizzes, but you do have a way of bringing in oblique thinking. Masterful planning, if true."

There had to be more to the plan, thought Kiki. What?

"With Chinese forces massed in the east, apparently preparing for an invasion of the U.S., the Russians would never see this coming," said Kennedy. "This move makes China the undisputed superpower in the world."

"That's troubling," said the president. "Would Russia resort to tactical nukes to take back their territory? Such a move could easily escalate."

"Tactical nukes could poison Russian soil for years. Their TNs aren't clean," stated Kennedy.

Nukes, thought Kiki. Could having those on the table be what scared the Russian command? Was this what the Director sensed?

General Edwards spoke up, "Sir, the logistics of supporting an invasion, even from Mongolia are difficult. Supply lines would be thousands of miles long."

"True," said Kennedy, "unless they are planning a two-pronged attack, one from China, west of Mongolia, and the other from the Black Sea. Maybe the troops massed at the ports are destined for the Black Sea?"

"Nice grasp of geometry and tactics," said the president. "Okay under that assumption, what should our response be?" There was silence. "Yeah, I haven't thought of anything either. All right, people, I need ideas and time frames. We'll telecom again tomorrow. Thanks."

Chapter Fifty-Three

October 15
Haifa, Israel

Ilia docked just before dawn. The shipment of twenty-liter containers, now labeled vaccine with a lot number and date was quickly stowed on the Chinese freighter. The crew was released, and within an hour, departed with its second in command as the new captain. After a hearty breakfast, Ilia headed for the Leonardo Hotel. They had a new assignment.

"A Cuban news team!" scoffed Zyra. "We are going to Moscow as a Cuban news team with Lieutenant Mendez?" She stared from the window of their suite at the harbor, her mind awhirl. She had mixed feelings about going that deeply into Russia. It would be incredibly dangerous. She turned to face Ilia.

The CIA agent nodded. "In a few days, we fly to Spain. We pick up our equipment, identification papers and passports. In Moscow, we will cover the press conference scheduled for next week. Vladimirov is expected to announce his plans for sending volunteers into Lithuania and Latvia to protect ethnic Russians from further persecution. Those Russian citizens are uniting to split off and form their own republics."

A news team in Russia, she wondered. "What is it we're to do as this news team?"

"We will be videotaping the news conference with very special equipment. If our mission is successful, it may change the whole dynamic between Russia and Eastern Europe."

"From merely videotaping a news conference? How does that happen?" asked Zyra.

"The equipment is very special. It comes with a trainer in Spain to see that we use it correctly."

Interesting, thought Zyra. "And why is Lieutenant Mendez to be with us?"

"He is our team leader. In addition to helping with the equipment, his skills will be useful for our departure. He is from Cuba."

"That will be valuable. My Spanish is good though with an accent – not enough that most

Russians would know. Sasha speaks Spanish, do you?"

Ilia nodded. "I spent a year in Madrid."

Zyra heard the hair dryer in the bathroom. It was such an ordinary sound compared to this conversation. Fifteen minutes later, Sasha emerged, now with dark brown hair. She looked good as a brunette, thought Zyra, but then she always looked good.

"Ah, Sasha you're finished," exclaimed Ilia. "We have a few days off. We could go see aunt Jasmin this afternoon."

Zyra was a little envious of the family that Sasha and Ilia had. She had none. "I think maybe I go to my old kibbutz."

"Oh, Zyra, come with us. I want you to meet Aunt Jasmin. Ilia and I are alive today because of her. When Mama and Papa arranged for Ilia and me to escape Russia, it was Aunt Jasmin who took us in. Mama's execution strengthened Aunt Jasmin's resolve to make us strong. It is we who must make those killers pay."

"But not today," said Ilia. "Come with us. You are part of our family. Let's push this world away for a day."

Chapter Fifty-Four

October 18
Casa Grande, Arizona

Miriam came out onto the patio. "Sorry to interrupt. With Brad and his family and Stephen and his family back in their homes, we have room here, if you'd care to stay. It would save a drive back to the National Guard base and you can continue to talk."

"Thank you, Mrs. Sabino. That's very gracious of you."

"I'll make up the guest rooms."

"It's wonderful of you to open up your home to us," said Ron.

"One thing we've learned from this crisis is to care for others," said Miriam. "See you in the morning." She closed the sliding glass door behind her.

"Wonderful mother you have, Nick," said Kennedy. She's special."

Nick nodded. Both his parents were. A pang over the loss for his father hit him.

Kiki saw it. Time to change the subject, she thought. "If we're right, after the Chinese troops ship out, how much time before they arrive in the Black Sea?" she asked.

"Guangzhou is the closest big port where we've seen troops. Transit time to Suez is five days. Another three days into the Black Sea," said David Kennedy.

"And the time for troops to arrive at the Mongolian border with Russia?" Ron asked.

"About the same," Kennedy said. "I expect the troops on the Chinese or Mongolian border would arrive first to draw any resistance out of Black Sea ports."

"And on the way to the oil fields is Koltsovo and its stock of weaponized smallpox," said Nick, remembering the Vector Institute. "Bio-warfare rears its ugly head again. Could those troops be the ones who were to receive the vaccine we hijacked?"

Slowly, David Kennedy nodded. "It's possible. Our theft of the shipment may have thrown off the schedule. The problem with the smallpox bioweapon is the gestation time between infection and when the disease strikes. To be effective, it must be distributed one to two weeks prior to the invasion," he said.

"Probably more like four weeks so it could spread," said Ron. "Let's table the bio-factor for a while. China could start a border skirmish to delay Russia's attack in Europe simply to buy time. That may be what they are offering Europe."

Kennedy smiled. "We could do the same by moving U.S. Naval forces, say a carrier group, just outside the Sea of Okhotsk. Russia would have to respond, and that means redeploying naval forces and air groups from the western border," he said. "The Sea of Okhotsk is Russian waters. To go into it would be considered an invasion, but there are no opposing forces."

"That would certainly get their attention," laughed Kiki.

"It would also aid China's real invasion," said Kennedy, in a somber voice.

"Yeah, I have a problem helping China become the sole super power in the world," said Ron.

Kiki listened to this discussion between the two government officials as world changing scenarios bounced back and forth. She shook her head at the thought of the fall of the U.S. from that lofty position.

"So what we're saying is that China is probably not considering a U. S. invasion," said Ron. "China's goal may be large chunks of Russia, particularly those with resources."

"Then what are our plans?" asked Kiki.

"If we do nothing, China and Russia battle it out. At first China will win simply because of the resources they have," noted David Kennedy. "Russia's European conquest plans collapse. Russia must counter China to regain the oil and gas reserves. From a logistics point, Russia will be able take back what they've lost, unless China mounts a major assault. From China to the Black Sea is a lot of territory to hold."

"True," said Kiki. "The joker in the deck is nuclear weapons." She couldn't let go of that niggling idea the Director had brought up.

"I do not doubt that Vladimirov will use nukes if he's losing," said Ron.

"Yeah," agreed Kennedy, "even if the Russian troops are devastated by a bio-attack. Perhaps more so then?"

"But would he use long-range weapons or just tactical?" posed Ron.

"Tactical are only good if forces are available to take advantage afterward, and they are clean nukes. Dirty nukes leave a mess for decades," said Kennedy.

"Maybe that's the point of the Chinese attack," noted Kiki.

"Yeah," said Ron. "If the Russians use tactical nukes on the invading Chinese, they lose their gas and oil reserves. The Russian economy completely collapses."

"China has been taking great pains to buddy up to the Middle East," said Kennedy. "They have bought oil and gas reserves there. The loss of Russian gas and oil would drive the prices sky high. Would Russia use long-range missiles and go after Beijing or Shanghai?" he posed. "That would escalate to total destruction for both of them."

"All fascinating thoughts and ideas," said Ron. "Let's meet in the morning and talk more before we conference with the president."

They said their goodnights and retired to their rooms.

In the dark, Nick and Kiki lay beside each other, fully awake.

"I still believe China has the U.S. in its sights. I just don't know how it will take place," said Nick. "They will make a move in the next few weeks."

Chapter Fifty-Five

October 21
Moscow, Russia

The Cuban news team were settling into their rooms after a grueling flight and an interminable immigration and customs experience. They had two days before Vladimirov's address, time to look around and fake some special interest pieces. In reality, they were scoping out an escape plan.

Their equipment was the expected big bulky camera, out of date by modern standards, but as new as would be used in Cuba. The autofocus on this camera used a laser to read distance. That was something Kiki would be familiar with as a sniper. They had learned everything about the equipment, including how to disassemble and reassemble it, making any needed repairs. They had taken instruction in being a news crew –

finding proper filming sites, lighting, conducting interviews and giving commentary.

Ilia took the umbrella to the roof of the hotel. Within seconds, it was assembled as their satellite link to David Kennedy. It was the appointed time.

"David, we're set up. Once we get Vladimirov's speech particulars out of the way tomorrow, we'll do some exploring and fake some public interest pieces. It will be our practice sessions with our Russian guide. He was assigned to us at immigration and sticks close." Ilia pressed the send button, and the message went out as a squirt transmission, impossible to intercept or decode, much less locate.

Seconds later, a light glowed on the satellite box. With a single earbud, Ilia pushed a button and listened. "Glad you're ready. Any problems?" asked Kennedy.

"Nothing unexpected has happened. We'll get the schedule and the press location assignment tomorrow. Being from Cuba has its perks. Only one guide has been assigned. We'll be able to shake him when necessary." Ilia pressed the send button.

"We're watching the situation on the western border with Latvia and the Chinese border to the east. The Chinese buildup has slowed Vladimirov's invasion plans, though he seems to be in a wait and see mode. We'll be meeting with the president tonight to present our plans. Extraction strategies for you are being formulated now. Your input will help. Talk to you same time tomorrow."

Ilia folded up the satellite system and returned to his room. Zyra and Sasha looked up as he entered. "Tomorrow we check out Red Square at the press section. We do some touring of Moscow, talk to people." They were acutely aware that the room must be bugged.

***

October 21
Camp David, Maryland

"What are our options for getting them out?" asked Carson, looking at David Kennedy. Ron was acutely aware of the danger the team in Russia faced. They'd been monitoring from Washington since the team's departure from Spain.

"They need to go either north or south," said General Edwards. "To the west are the troops. To the east is far too much land with nothing. We were able to fly the Anatov east before because it was never expected. But now, Russia is on high alert. Trying to repeat that would be very risky."

"Either north or south then. We're going to have to supply help," said David Kennedy. "To the north, we'd require naval help. We'd be in Ivan's backyard."

"Even using a sub would be risky," agreed General Edwards.

"That leaves egress to the south," said Ron. "We have to get them from Moscow to a border. How?"

"Rail is out," stated Kennedy. "It's got no options once they are on the train. Road is possible, but it would take days to get to the border. That's a lot of time to set up a search and arrest plan. It has to be air, small plane."

"But no small planes have the range to reach the border. They would have to land and refuel," said Ron.

"We'll start looking," said David Kennedy. "Some planes have the range, but they'd have to steal one. The small commercial airport on the edge of Moscow is the best place to start."

Chapter Fifty-Six

October 23
Moscow, Russia

Zyra looked at the crowd filling Red Square through the viewer of the video camera. There were at least 100,000 people. The weather had cooperated. It was a sunny and crisp afternoon, a good day for Moscow this time of year. A roar arose as officials stepped out onto the dais. A solid line of security surrounded the podium. The fit form of Vladimirov was unmistakable. Through the viewer's magnification, she clearly saw his eyes take in the cheering crowd. He smiled at the adulation.

Behind her, she knew Sasha, Ilia and Richard were checking out the people, watching their guide. Vladimirov stepped to the podium, raising his hands for quiet. The roar increased then tapered off. There was a tap on her shoulder. She centered the crosshairs of the viewer on Vladimirov's eyes and pressed the red stud of the camera. He stumbled backward, hands flying at his eyes as he fell. The laser range finder was much more. It had done its job. Zyra lowered the camera to the shouts of pandemonium. The phalanx of security moved out into the crowd and the press section, pushing everybody back. People surged forward. In the confusion, the Cuban news team turned to retreat.

"Something has happened to the president," Ilia said to their guide, pointing to the balcony. He moved forward. The four team members threaded their way back into the crowd, losing him.

At the van, they quickly changed clothes and drove away from the square to the sound of sirens. The small business airport was twenty kilometers away, the traffic on the road was light. Thirty minutes later they were in the air, winging their way south. Ilia sent the signal to Kennedy of success, so far.

***

Camp David
October 23

"That's the code, Mr. President," said Kennedy. "They're on the plane."

The president let out a breath. The conference room that had seemed so stuffy moments before was a little roomier. "Did the laser work?" he asked.

"The Russians are being very quiet about what happened," said George Pickering. "We're getting news from the hospital that he was temporarily blinded by a bright light. That laser did the job. His eyes are burned out."

"God!" exclaimed the president. "We've blinded a head of state. That seems more immoral than assassinating him."

"We did that, but it's a long drawn out process, not quick," said Ron Carson. "In the oligarchy of Russia, the sharks are already circling, sensing the weakened leader."

"Yes, I know," said the president. "Vladimirov will hold them off, perhaps for months. But in the end, his enemies will come in for the kill."

"There will be a struggle for power," said Pickering, "perhaps lasting years before a new leader takes the helm for a lengthy time. We've blunted the European conquest. The internal battle will take precedence. The commanding general will struggle to maintain control of the armed forces within the country."

David Kennedy's phone chirped. He was never to be disturbed while with the president. He looked at the caller and answered. His head nodded several times, clicked off and turned to the president. "Mr. President, Chinese forces are driving toward Koltsovo. The main body has crossed the border. Advance forces parachuted into important objectives. That includes airports."

"What about Sochi, the one our team is heading for?" asked Ron.

Kennedy nodded. "Sochi was one of the first because of the airport and the seaport. I suspect the Chinese troop ship is en route there. We're looking for alternate sites now. The Gazprom jet we took needs a runway at least 2000 feet long and not dirt. Our list of alternatives and the Chinese list of targets are the same."

"Mr. President," said George Pickering, "we followed the Chinese freighter after it left Haifa. It rendezvoused with the Chinese troop ship six days ago. That ship is in the Black Sea now."

"So," began the president, "our team is heading for an airport occupied by Chinese paratroopers and where a Chinese troop ship will dock. Does that sum it up? What are our options?" He looked from face to face.

"We could try to divert the plane to Ukraine, but they might shoot down a Russian plane, regardless if it's civilian or not," stated General Tom Edwards.

"We could suggest to the pilot the plane put down on the highway and the team go into escape and evade while we mount a rescue," suggested Ron Carson. "It'll be dark there in under an hour."

"Ilia knows the area," said David Kennedy. "He could hide the team until we get help to them."

"Help from where?" asked the president. "They were to board the pleasure yacht we had in the port and sail for Odeso. I doubt the Chinese will allow that now."

"Sir, we still have the Carl Vinson task force within range. We could dispatch a tanker from Turkey to keep the rescue helios and escort F-35s in the air," said General Edwards.

"Okay, that's Plan A. Let's go with that," said the president. "Start working on Plan B now."

Chapter Fifty-Seven

October 23
Russian airspace

"Ilia, Zyra, Sasha, there's a message coming in." Mendez routed it through the intercom.

"Richard, David Kennedy here. Sochi is compromised. Chinese troops have taken it. Land wherever you can. Go E & E. We'll set up an extraction. Stay in contact with us via squirt satellite transmission."

"Roger. Out," said Mendez, cutting the connection. "Come up to the cockpit. Escape and evade is Ilia's and my area of expertise. We need to make preparations." Zyra took the copilot's seat while Ilia and Sasha crowded the doorway.

"Get our com gear and other necessities secured next to the door. Search for weapons and cold weather clothing. Gazprom probably has some onboard. We'll be running in the dark, so put on appropriate gear. Take blankets. I'm going to set us down on the best strip of road I can find. Ilia, stay and help me with that. You know the area. Move, people. We'll be there in fifteen minutes and we can't circle. The Chinese might shoot us down."

"Come in from the east," said Ilia. "The Russians had AA batteries to the north and west of the airport. Thirty-miles south of Sochi is Kholodnaia. October Street intersects the E 60 just north. We'll land on October Street on a south-southeast heading. That road is lightly traveled and straight. We can get to the forest, about five-hundred yards away. I have a safe house north of the city, only a few miles hike. We will stay there until extraction plans are made."

Richard nodded. He was not a fan of emergency landings, especially in Russia. Ilia pointed to airport beacons five miles to the south-southwest. "Sochi airport." The runway lights were off. Traffic on the roads was light, no doubt at the order of the invaders. Good for us, he thought. "Three minutes," he announced. "Brace for hard landing."

He and Ilia tightened their harnesses as they dumped fuel. In the fading light, Richard saw October Street. He nosed down sharply. It had no traffic, but the E 60 ahead had several trucks on it. A power line loomed. Richard had to go under it or run out of straight road. The landing was hard. A loud crunch signaled the collapse of the port landing gear. The plane slued, hitting a power pole and shearing off a wing. The tail broke away. He heard someone scream. The silence was abrupt as the plane stopped.

Richard looked out the windshield, something wet was in his eyes, blood from a cut. The nose of the plane pointed to the E 60. To his horror, he saw one of the big trucks stop less than five-hundred yards away. It was a troop carrier, and soldiers began jumping out of it. "We have to get out of here." He grabbed Ilia and shook him. Ilia's eyes focused. Richard pointed toward the running soldiers heading for them.

He and Ilia ran into the cabin. Sasha was struggling to get out of her harness. Zyra was unconscious, blood dribbling from her forehead. Ilia used a knife to cut Sasha free. Richard released Zyra's harness and threw her over his shoulder. Ilia and Sasha grabbed their gear and ran out of the gaping hole that used to be the back of the plane. Richard stumbled and went down. By the time he got up, the barrel of an AK

74 was pointed between his eyes. Slowly, he raised his hands.

From the trees, Ilia and Sasha watched the soldiers carry Zyra, Richard marching beside the litter. Turning into the woods, they hurried away unseen.

Chapter Fifty-Eight

October 24
Camp David

"Shit!" exclaimed the president. "What now?" he asked looking from General Edwards to David Kennedy.

"We're having the extraction team stand down. Until we know more, we can't send anybody in. Ilia and Sasha are safe for the moment," said Kennedy. "Once we find out where Zyra and Lieutenant Mendez are being held, we'll put together a new Plan A."

***

October 24
Gorodskaya Bolnitsa #7 Hospital

Zyra was still unconscious, a huge bandage on her head. Richard also had a bandage, but a smaller one. He eyed the Chinese guard watching them, rifle at the ready. Something was wrong. The man's skin had large reddish-black blotches, and sweat beaded his brow. The whites of his eyes were red with blood. He swayed.

Richard had been briefed on smallpox. This man had the hemorrhagic form, and maybe four days to live. If he had it, so did a lot of other people. Behind him, there was a commotion. The guard remained frozen. A gurney wheeled past the door. On it was another soldier, this one wearing the insignia of a general. Red blotches covered his face, but not nearly as bad as their guard. The invaders were infected.

Zyra stirred. Richard went to her side. Her eyes fluttered open but didn't focus. He put a hand on her shoulder. She looked at the hand then at him. He smiled at her. "We'll be okay," he said in Spanish. He watched her eyes close.

A Chinese officer entered, a captain, Richard saw. "Who are you?" the officer barked in English.

Richard looked at him. "We are the Cuban Press Corps here to cover Vladimirov's speech," Richard said in Spanish. He gestured toward his jacket with their press badges.

The officer went to look. "You do not speak English?" he said, inspecting the credentials.

Richard shrugged, holding his hands out and shaking his head. The officer left. Twenty minutes later another officer appeared, a lieutenant.

"So, you are Cuban," he said in Spanish.

"Si'," said Richard.

"What are you doing on a plane that crashed on the road?" inquired the officer.

"After something happened to Vladimirov, soldiers started rounding everybody up. We fled and took that plane. We ran out of fuel. I had to land on the road."

"There were just the two of you?" asked the officer.

Richard nodded. "The rest of our party got separated during the chaos at the speech. Guards were shooting tear gas and clubbing everyone. We were obviously not Russian and had to flee."

"We will see," said the officer. He left.

With Cuba as allies, the Chinese would not kill them, thought Richard. With the fog of war, they might not check the authenticity of their credentials at once. Ilia and Sasha had not been captured.

Chapter Fifty-Nine

October 25
Gorodskaya Bolnitsa #7 Hospital

Richard awoke as a doctor in a white coat, a stethoscope around his neck entered. Morning sunlight streamed through the window. His head throbbed, but as his eyes focused, he realized the doctor was Ilia, who held a finger to his lips.

"I thought they'd take you to the nearest hospital," Ilia said in Spanish. "Now that I know you and Zyra are here, we can put together extraction plans. Are you both mobile, can you walk?"

"I can. Zyra's still shaky. Ilia, there's more. These Chinese troops are infected with hemorrhagic smallpox."

Ilia began feigning a physical examination of Richard as he talked. "Yeah, I noticed most of them looked sick when I arrived. Looks like the vaccine I took to the Chinese ship worked."

"What do you mean?" asked Richard.

"You don't think I'd give them real vaccine, do you? The cargo we loaded onto the ship was the active strain developed by the Russians to use as a weapon. Their inoculation program infected their own troops."

Richard smiled. What poetic justice. "There's more. A high-ranking general was brought in last night. If we take him with us, we might get valuable information."

"Where is he?"

"Down the hall is all I know," said Richard.

"I'll check it out. Be back to you after I relay the information and we get a plan." Ilia left, a chart in his hand.

Richard felt a glimmer of hope they'd get out of this. He looked at the soldier guarding them. He was different from the one last night, but he had reddish-black splotches on his skin, too.

***

October 25
Camp David

"Mr. President, we heard from our agent, Ilia," said CIA Director David Kennedy. "He's located Zyra and Lieutenant Mendez at a local hospital. It's remote enough we can plan an extraction."

"That's good news," the president exclaimed.

"There's more," added Kennedy. "Many of the Chinese troops are infected with hemorrhagic smallpox. Obviously, their vaccination program backfired, as you foresaw. This invasion may be only slightly longer than The Bay of Pigs." The joke fell flat.

"We got a bonus," said Ron Carson. "A high-ranking Chinese general is at the same hospital. If we bring him out, we might gain valuable intel."

"Okay, what's your plan?" asked the president.

"Sir, we're going to keep it simple," stated David Kennedy. "We'll land a helicopter at the hospital with our SEAL team disguised as doctors and staff. They're going to go in and take Zyra and Richard out as patients. We'll go after the general the same way."

"Will it really be that simple?" asked the president.

"We'll stage a diversion in Sochi to draw troops away. The Chinese have set up headquarters in the government offices. A drone will rocket it. We'll radio that Russians are counterattacking from the north," said General Edwards. "We'll also send out orders for all available Chinese troops to move into Sochi. F-35s will be orbiting just out of radar range. Any resistance remaining at the hospital will be dealt with."

"Not bad," said the president. "It just might work."

Chapter Sixty

October 26
Camp David

"Mr. President, it went well," shouted Ilia over the throbbing of the helicopter. "We've got Zyra and Lieutenant Mendoza. We also have the Chinese general. That's the good news. The bad news is the general has only a few days to live. He knows it, so he won't have any incentive to talk. Interrogation will be difficult. I don't think we can break him before he dies."

"Mr. President, we might try Nick Sabino and Katherine Russell for the interrogation," said Ron Carson. "The C-17 with their equipment is in Haifa. We could fly them out tonight, they'd be there by tomorrow."

"You can't have a contagious man going anywhere," said the president. "Once that helicopter lands on Carl Vinson, it must be isolated. The crew has been vaccinated, but we can't take chances. How do we get the general onto the C-17?"

"Sir," said General Edwards, "We could divert the chopper to the Naval Support base at Deveselu, Romania. The C-17 can land there. We'll wheel the chopper onto the C-17. No contact with anyone."

"I like that a lot better," said the president. "Contact Sabino and Russell. Put them on fast flights to Deveselu. Have that C-17 meet them there. If the report on the general is correct, the clock is ticking."

***

October 26
Casa Grande, Arizona

Nick's phone chirped, waking him instantly. Who would be calling him at this hour? "Hello."

"Nick, this is Ron Carson. I've got an emergency, and we need your help. A chopper is on the way to pick you up. It'll be in your driveway in thirty minutes. I'll meet you at the Pinal National Guard Airpark." The phone disconnected.

"Who was that?" asked Kiki in a husky voice.

"Looks like we have a job. Better pack. We're leaving here in half an hour." They both stumbled from the bed.

The clattering of the helicopter woke Miriam. Nick explained that he and Kiki were needed. He turned, and they hurried toward the chopper, ducking under the rotating blades. Thirty minutes later they landed. It was dark and chilly standing in the open hangar door facing the runway.

Within minutes, a Gulfstream 650 landed. Fuel trucks awaited as it taxied to the hangar. The door opened and Ron Carson waved for them to come aboard.

"Nice ride," said Kiki looking at the luxury accommodations of the aircraft. "Are you trying to impress us?" The plane began to accelerate, and they hastily sat, buckling their seatbelts. It was amazingly quiet.

Ron laughed. "No, but this is one of the fastest passenger planes available. We need an interrogation. We captured a high-ranking general in the Chinese army invading Russia. We must know what their plans are."

"What's the rush?" Nick asked.

"He has smallpox, the hemorrhagic form. He's got four days to live, and little incentive to talk. We need your help."

"Where are we going?" asked Kiki. "Are we in danger from the contagion?"

"No, no danger. You've been inoculated. We're meeting the C-17 with your equipment at the Naval Support Base at Deveselu, Romania. The helicopter carrying the general will meet us there. An interpreter is waiting."

"Chinese," noted Nick. "I've never questioned a Communist Chinese before."

"Try to get some rest," Ron gestured at the fully reclining seats with blankets and pillows. "There's a shower in the back, if you want one." He pointed to a waiting steward. "Cheryl can cook up anything you want." A slender woman waved at them from the back of the plane. "You better take advantage of the rest and luxury. Once we board the C-17, it'll be balls to the wall.

Chapter Sixty-One

October 27
Naval Support Base, Deveselu, Romania

Nick checked over the isolation chamber to assure it was operational and the necessary drugs were available. The roar of the engines and the vibration of the plane were concerns, but the sound compartment worked on the ship before. Satisfied, he motioned the SEAL team to wheel the gurney from the sealed helicopter, now resting in the plane's huge bay. It had taken the ground crew at Deveselu only thirty minutes to fold the rotors back and roll the helicopter aboard. In less than an hour, they were in the air. Their destination was clear airspace, not a landing site.

The SEAL team was still clad in medical garb, white coats and scrubs. The skin of the unconscious figure on the gurney was now covered in blackish blotches. The disease had progressed rapidly. They didn't have days to question him. Nick decided to change his prep procedure. He did a spinal block to eliminate the pain from the disease. With the IVs inserted, they eased the general into the chamber. Brine began to circulate as the lid was lowered.

Turning to check the monitors, Nick found Zyra standing behind him, her head still bandaged. "Glad to have you back," he said.

"I am happy to be here." Sasha hovered behind Zyra like a helicopter mom. "I am interested to see how you open up this general."

Nick looked at the monitors. Sitting in his chair with the laptop before him, he increased the stimulants, watching the heart rate and breathing. Ron Carson turned on his recorder as the general awoke.

Through an interpreter, Nick said, *"Welcome, General Zhing."*

"Who is that?" asked the general.

"I cannot blame you for not recognizing me. You were barely a child when I began the new China."

"You are Chairman Mao? Why can I not see you?"

"We have no bodies in this place. It is where our minds go after life on Earth."

"I am dead? This disease killed me?"

"It did. How did you become infected?"

"The vaccine that was supposed to immunize us so we could use smallpox to sanitize the parts of Russia we captured was the disease. I fear it may destroy our army. We vaccinated not only our invasion force, but also the Red Guard in the provinces. Our plan was to cleanse the areas of discontents so our loyal followers could take over."

"It is the influence of religion and the Western World that has contaminated the minds of our people."

"We struck a blow at them. The smallpox was released in America, infecting the large cities. To control it, they withdrew their armies from overseas assignments and deployed them domestically. We also had our ally North Korea attack their electrical grid, disabling their infrastructure. America's economy is in ruins and will remain so for years. In that time, we are going to send assistance in the form of food and medical aid. Those teams will help, but they will also buy contaminated lands and failed businesses. We will buy America at fire-sale prices. Our people will be benevolent in every way."

"It is good to see you are following my instructions. You must make the people your allies, and you must be better than their government to gain their loyalty. Once you have their hearts and minds, you will rule."

"It is especially easy in America, where our people can be elected and become the government. Our invasion of America is to be with silk and a feather. Our aid forces were inoculated with this vaccine. I fear for them."

"Rest for now. We will talk again."

Nick increased the sedatives, watching the general's vital signs slow. He wasn't sure the general would survive for another session.

"We got the proof we needed," said Ron, holding up the recorder. "I'll send it to the president. We'll set up a conference in a few hours." He rushed from the sound chamber.

Nick and Kiki were alone with the general. They both stared at the isolation chamber.

"Whatever we say about the Director, America's devil is in that chamber," said Kiki.

"What a monstrous plot. Millions of people will die before this is over. And for what?"

Kiki's mind tingled. She looked at Nick. He nodded. It was coming.

"Ooh, Nick, Katherine. What a feast awaits me. Perhaps you do not realize what is coming, but I can put together the picture. War on an unprecedented scale is about to start, and you have been instrumental in creating this banquet for me. Thank you."

"I'm sure you're welcome," sneered Kiki. "We certainly never intended to help you."

"I know. That is what makes you so fun. The harder you try not to help me, the more you do. The flavor of your distaste for me is a tangy spice. With the nuclear holocaust coming and the disease that has spread death, fear and hatred abound. Tata."

Kiki felt like weeping. This beast, this thing that fed on the human emotions of hatred and fear would never leave them alone. Nick's arm pulled her close.

"We will survive. We will triumph."

Chapter Sixty-Two

October 27
Situation Room, Camp David

"The question is what do we do now that we have the proof?" asked the president.

"We bomb the hell out of the Chinese!" exclaimed General Edwards.

David Kennedy, George Pickering and Athena Brown nodded agreement.

"Mr. President," said Secretary of State Volgyi, "they need to be hurt for what they did, but the risk of a total nuclear exchange is too great to just send the nukes."

"I agree," said the president.

"Mr. President, what's the status of the Russians? Where's the Chinese invasion now?" asked Ron Carson, his face filling the monitor on the wall.

"The Russians are pulling forces from their European borders, sending them to defend against the Chinese," reported David Kennedy. "Vladimirov maintains control as there could be no opposition to defending the gas and oil fields."

George Pickering spoke up, "The NSA monitors are picking up a lot traffic. His opponents are preparing for a campaign after that invasion is repelled. Vladimirov will not have the strength to hold to his plan to invade Eastern Europe. Already there is open criticism of his leaving Eastern Russia defenseless for his vision of grandeur. The cracks are forming."

"The unknown question," said General Edwards, "is the effect of the smallpox on all troops. China's invasion was brought to a halt by the massive loss of forces. Not just the Chinese army has been hit by the plague. The residents are dying in great numbers. If the Russian army lumbers into the area, they will become infected. Koltsovo holds the only vaccine, and the Chinese paratroopers hold that. Unfortunately, for them, the Chinese army driving toward them has also suffered great losses. Their support may not arrive in time."

"Pardon me if I don't shed tears for either of them," said the president. "Mr. Sabino, how confident are you of the accuracy of the information from the General Zheng?"

"Mr. President, he believed everything he told us. Any falsehoods were fed to him."

"Could further questioning lend credibility?" asked David Kennedy.

"I don't believe he will last through another session. His body temperature has risen to the point he is hallucinating. We're trying to keep him cool within the chamber, but his end is near."

"Did the general say anything about the agenda for the Convention of the Communist Party next week?"

"No, sir. I didn't know to ask."

"Thank you, Mr. Sabino, and thanks to your team. Job well done. We may need you again."

"Any time, Mr. President."

"Ron, stay with us, please."

"Okay, so from what the CIA has determined, the Chinese National Conference next week involves all 3000 Chinese Communist Party officials from the entire country. We must assume the President will say something about the invasion and the plagues. He will blame them on the United States, of course. Let's table the Chinese and Russians for a moment," said the president. "The North Koreans deserve some attention."

"They were hired by the Chinese to destroy our infrastructure. They did it. David, what assets do we have in place that know of this attack?"

"We had one asset who was involved. He and his superior officer were recently promoted and moved from the electronic warfare section to the ballistic missile section. They needed stronger programming capability."

"That doesn't bode well," said the president. "It is time to become more proactive."

Chapter Sixty-Three

October 29
Casa Grande, Arizona

"Thanks for picking us up," said Nick to Brad. The desert view flew past as the sheriff's cruiser sped along I-10. Few cars were on the road. Both Nick and Kiki dozed. At Miriam's house, they awoke.

"Sorry we weren't much company," said Kiki, getting out of the car with her meager duffle. The front door opened and Miriam came out, a rosy color to her face and full of hugs for them.

"You kids go outside," she said. "I'll bring refreshments."

The view from the patio was of the valley below. The late afternoon sun cast a golden glow over the desert. Lights began to come on. At the edges of the city, the tents in the refugee camps glowed.

"Nick, you and Kiki look like you've been rode hard and put away wet," said Brad. "That must have been a grueling trip."

"We've been on planes for five days," said Kiki. "These were not commercial jets, so the seats were bad, and the food and beverage service really sucked." They all laughed.

"Can you tell me anything about it?" Brad looked from Kiki to Nick.

"It was a four country whirlwind tour with no tour," said Kiki, with a wry smile.

"Brad," said Nick, "someday we'll be able to tell you. I will say that the foreign problems we faced are much smaller now."

Miriam appeared with cold beers and iced tea for Brad.

"How are things here?" asked Nick, changing the subject.

"CG's doing okay. It's not back to normal, but we've got power. Our residents are getting along with the refugees. Everybody is pulling together. Refugees pitched in, and we have winter food crops in the ground. Most of them are still living in the tent cities surrounding us. We're getting food, water and clothing shipments in from the National Guard."

"Some of these poor people are really nice," said Miriam. "I'm enjoying the opportunity to teach again. I haven't done that since soon after your father and I were married."

"Left alone, we'd be fine." Brad frowned.

"The problem is," he continued, "that more refugees keep coming, mostly from Phoenix. Despite the quarantine of California, smallpox struck. Added to the lack of power and water, Phoenix is a nightmare. Even with the army, law and order has broken down. Sections of the city are controlled by armed gangs, eager to defend their territory. Soldiers have been sniped at. We've heard rumors that there's a strongman in California trying to organize the gangs into an army and create a new nation."

What was going on? How did it get this bad, wondered Kiki. She shook her head slowly, not understanding. The haven the United States had always been was collapsing.

"We've begun to patrol our own perimeters to keep out people. A couple of gang members got into our camps. They wanted to start a branch gang here, trying to recruit from the refugees."

"What happened to them?" asked Kiki.

"They got shot," stated Brad, adding nothing else.

"Is the military calling up reservists and recalling retired military?" asked Kiki.

Brad nodded. "I've received requests to help locate vets. Your names were on the list. You're to report tomorrow."

They were called, thought Kiki. That wouldn't be bad. Who they would be fighting would be horrible. Nick and Kiki looked at Brad, their mouths open. It sounded like Afghanistan, only the enemy was Americans.

"Does this mean you'll be leaving again?" asked Miriam. "You just arrived. That doesn't seem right."

Nick thought about calling in a favor from Ron or the president. He rejected it. They all had a duty.

Chapter Sixty-Four

October 30
Florence, Arizona

The morning bus ride from the National Guard Armory brought back memories of Kiki's enlistment. The passengers were a lot older. The bus was heading for Florence, the home of the Arizona State Prison and a National Guard Training center. Unlike Kiki's enlistment, there would not be six weeks of basic training followed by another six weeks of Advanced Infantry Training. They would be evaluated. Those most ready, meaning physically fit and recently separated from the military, would be deployed immediately.

At reception, they lined up before tables with alphabetic listings. Nick and Kiki were in line at the R-T table. The sergeant asked Kiki's name, typed it in. As he read the file, his eyebrows rose. "Welcome back, Sergeant Russell. It's an honor to meet you." Several of the soldiers at the other tables glanced at her. He pointed. "Please proceed through that door." As Kiki walked away, she heard Nick give his name.

The physical was perfunctory, the medic stoic. Fifteen minutes later, she exited through another door in her new and poorly fitting uniform. Over her shoulder was her duffle bag with all her worldly possessions. "Sergeant Russell, report to bus number six outside," said another soldier.

As she walked toward the bus in the noon sun, a shout came from behind her. It was Nick! Their hug was intense. "Bus six?" she asked. He nodded. A ray of light sprang up.

They sat together, duffels in the overhead rack, sack lunches in hand. The bus held eighteen passengers. A lean man with a hard face, thinning gray hair and wearing lieutenant insignia stepped on.

"I'm Lieutenant Harvey. None of us are new recruits, so you know the drill. You people are assigned to me because your former military jobs are what we need. We're going to retake Los Angles. For those of you who don't know, it's a mess. Gangs have taken over parts, and they are making up their own laws. Some of these gangs are outlaw motorcycle gangs, others are drug gangs, both domestic and Mexican. You might think this is a civil action. It is not. I've been there, and I've been in Afghanistan. The only difference is these guys don't wear black kaftans. Otherwise, it's the same. There have been beheadings and soldiers killed, so they aren't kidding around. They have chosen to overthrow the legitimate government. These guys raided armories so they're armed. This is a military action."

The lieutenant shifted his stance and looked from face to face around the bus. "An Afghan vet, Captain Sean Gallen is trying to pull the loose factions together under his command. He's been brutal with opposition. Once he gets them united, we'll have a full-blown war on our hands. Get some sleep now. We'll hit the ground running after we cross the California border."

Nick and Kiki held each other tightly. As they headed into the setting sun, both wondered what lay ahead.

The tanks across the highway west of Palm Springs at Cabazon were a blow of reality. After passing through the gate, an armored personnel carrier accompanied them. The only light penetrating the darkness were vehicles and the distant glow of fires. Kiki felt they were descending into the pit of hell.

The Riverside City College had been taken over as a military command post. The air smelled of smoke and burned meat. Lieutenant Harvey led them to a briefing room. It had been a small lecture hall. "Welcome home. We're bunking in the dorm next door, two to a room. Pick out a bunk. Stow your gear and report back here." He led them down a hall to a large cafeteria. "The mess hall is open twenty-four/seven. Get chow and meet me back in the briefing room in twenty minutes." The food was typical Army. It didn't take twenty minutes to eat.

"People, we leave in an hour for a night recon. Pick up weapons and gear at the armory. Sabino, you hook up with the medevac crew in the parking lot. Anyone with sniper experience?" Beside Kiki, one other hand went up.

"Sergeant Russell, he's your spotter. Pick out one other for your team. As soon as you have weapons and night vision, come back here."

"Dismissed!"

Most of the soldiers took the weapon issued to them. Kiki got to choose. These weapons were from Afghanistan, used but in good condition. The armorer watched her looking at the various weapons. "I'm looking, for an AR-10 in .25-06 caliber. Have anything like that?" she asked the armorer.

Few people talked to him, much less asked for a specific weapon. He peered at her closely. "Say," he rubbed his grizzly chin, "aren't you K, you know, Sergeant K from Afghanistan?" She nodded. "C'mon back here. I may have what you want." He unlocked another vault. "You don't know me. I'm Coots. You saved my ass in the Sandbox. We were pinned down by a heavy machinegun. They were chipping away our cover. It was only a matter of time. You blasted right through their armor with some sort of explosive round. Splashed 'em all."

"It was my Barrett 50," Kiki said.

"You want another? I got one."

"Hold it for me. Let me see what the terrain is like."

"Yeah, I'll put that aside. Aaah. Here's that AR 10. It's got a twelve-power variable scope with laser rangefinder. Got a night vision adaptor for it, too."

"You got a laser bore sight?" Kiki asked. "I need to at least check the sights before I go out."

"Yeah. C'mon. We'll go outside. Wait'll the guys hear that you're with us. Say, what happened to you?"

"Don't go there," said Kiki, her tone making it final.

"Yeah, Okay, sorry."

Outside, Kiki slipped the laser bore sight into the chamber of the AR 10. She lay in a prone position, gun on the bipod and aimed at a spot on a dark hulk of a car. The rangefinder indicated it was four hundred yards away. That was her zero point. She adjusted the scope until the laser dot was in the crosshairs. It would have to do until she could get to a range.

"Coots, I need a special suppressor with an extended tube. Can you get me that?"

"Yeah, no problem."

Kiki was in sniper mode, just like Afghanistan. But this wasn't a foreign country, or was it? Maybe it was. She'd see very soon.

Chapter Sixty-Five

October 31
Missile Control Center, North Korea

First Sergeant Kwang Ryang smoked quietly on the roof of the Missile Control Center. The wind whipped falling snowflakes about his face. He looked around to ensure he was alone. Few times in a man's life did he have to make a decision of the magnitude Kwang faced. Sliding a loose brick from the wall, he removed the cigarette-pack-sized black plastic box. Nervously, he glanced around again. At the push of a button, a small light glowed red. He pushed the button three times in rapid succession. The light turned green. He'd done it. Kwang replaced the transmitter dead brick. He had three hours to get his family away from the city and to the extraction point on the coast.

U.S.S. George Bush

"Sir, the signal just came through," said the signals operator.

Captain Roberts turned to his second in command. "Launch the drones."

On the deck, the engines of two black angular stealth-drones wound to a high-pitched screech. They rocketed off the carrier under the force of the electromotive catapult. Roberts watched them clear the deck, dip toward the sea before gaining altitude. They circled once and turned west. He hadn't been told of their destination, only to have them loaded with smart bombs, big ones. He could guess where they were going. Someone was in for a world of hurt.

Roberts went to his communications officer. "Send a secure squirt to Washington they're away."

Washington, D.C.
Situation Room

"Mr. President, they're on the way," said General Edwards.

"How long to target?" asked the president.

"Three hours," answered the general.

Three hours, thought the president. The face of the world will change. How, was the question. So much depended on that Korean agent, Kwang Ryang. "General, raise the DEFCON level to three. I don't want to alarm the Russians or the Chinese, but we have to be ready in case Kwang Ryang wasn't able to complete his mission."

"Yes, sir."

"You have the satellites in place?" The president realized he was asking nervous questions. He was nervous.

"Yes, sir."

The monitor on the wall was real-time from the drones. In the upper corners heading, speed, and time to target displayed. Gray waves with white mares' tails passed beneath.

In the monitor, the president saw the line of the coast. The view split. One drone turned north, the other south. The scene was hypnotizing. He saw no sign that the drones had been detected. Radar scans blipped, but the stealth mode of the drones kept the signature as small as birds. They wouldn't be noticed. The time to target switched from minutes to the seconds level. Crosshairs centered on a white building. The building disappeared in a blinding flash.

Twice more, the drones circled back and hit the rubble that had been the North Korean Technology Center. It was a smoking crater.

"Boo," said General Edwards.

The president looked at him.

"It is Halloween," explained the general with a smile.

Chapter Sixty-Six

October 31
Missile Control Center, North Korea

Captain Gun Rahn searched for First Sergeant Kwang Ryang. He was gone. It didn't matter; Gun would initiate the order to launch the intercontinental ballistic missiles. The destruction of the DPRK Tech Center was the America's response to the cyber-attack. The Premiere had ordered the launch.

Captain Rahn opened the silo lids. When the green light indicated they were open, he flipped up the launch switch covers. The red buttons stared at him. This was a war they could not win. He hesitated, then pushed all four.

Outside, four balls of fire with slender missiles atop rose into the air. It was done. The fifty-kiloton nuclear warheads were on the way.

Washington, D.C.
The Situation Room

"Mr. President, our satellite picked up the North Korean's launch," said General Edwards.

"Put the course tracking on the screen," said the president.

A map of the Korean Peninsula appeared. Four lines traced the path of the missiles. This was it, thought the president. The antiballistic missile system was poised to take them out if needed.

"Aren't you going to shoot them down?" cried Sharon Volgyi.

The president held up a hand, his eyes glued to the monitor. The traces began to arc south and west.

Missile Control Center, DPRK

Captain Gun Rahn watched the missiles on the radar. Something was wrong. Instead of heading east, they were going south and west. He hurried to the self-destruct buttons. Glancing back at the radar screen, he checked to see if their courses had changed. They hadn't. He pushed one self-destruct button. A blip disappeared. He pushed another. Nothing happened. He pushed it again. Nothing happened. Panic rose as he pushed the third button. A blip disappeared. Rahn felt some relief. He pushed the fourth button. Nothing happened. He pounded on the buttons. The missiles continued on their way.

Where were they going? Rahn called up the targeting coordinates on his computer screen. "Aaaah!" he screamed. One was going toward Russia, the other toward China. The communication module on each missile was disabled. He couldn't change the targeting, he couldn't blow them up.

Washington, D.C.
The Situation Room

Two missile tracks remained on the screen.
"Where are they headed?" asked Sharon Volgyi, her eyes wide.
"Let's watch," said the president, a grim smile on his face.

Chinese President Qiang Min held up his hands for quiet as he looked over the hall filled with delegates. He had both good and bad news to announce. Their invasion of Russia to claim the gas and oil fields was proceeding, slowed by the illness. The purge of dissidents from the outlying provinces was underway though the illness rate among the Red Guard was high. Somehow, the smallpox contagion had gotten away from them. He need not tell them that part.

From the wing, his assistant motioned he had an important message. Qiang angrily shook him off. This speech was more important. He had to reassure these representatives that China was on the right course – led by him.

Five times, he was interrupted by applause. At last, he walked to the wings. His assistant handed him a message. He looked, then looked again. This couldn't be right! The assistant handed him a phone.

"North Korea fired a nuclear missile at us?" he screamed. "Where is it aimed?" His face paled. There wasn't even time for him to go to a shelter.

Washington, D.C.
The Situation Room

Silently, the president watched the trace of one missile impact over Beijing. He felt no joy as millions of people died. The other track continued west, finally detonating over Koltsovo.

"How did that happen?" asked Secretary of State Sharon Volgyi.

"Obviously, something was wrong with their targeting system," smirked General Edwards. "Maybe the parts were made in China."

"Go to DEFCON 4," said the president. "We don't know what the Russians or the Chinese will do. Now that the detonations have occurred, it would be our normal response. Put a call through to Vladimirov. I want to assure him we didn't do it."

"Their own systems will show that the missiles originated in North Korea," said General Edwards. "We will reiterate that point."

"Place another call to China. I want to assure whoever is in charge we did not shoot those missiles." Finding who was in charge now might be difficult, thought the president.

Chapter Sixty-Seven

October 31
Riverside California.

They were driving dark, using night vision to weave their way through the stalled and abandoned cars blocking the freeway. A deuce-and-a-half with a blade on the front led the convoy, pushing the heaps aside. Their goal was the major intersection of I-605 and I-10. It had been barricaded to prevent forces from entering LA. Kiki and her team set up 400 yards away on a tower. Smoke hung in the air. Night vision was barely acceptable at these distances. Through her NV, she watched her unit advance. A shot flashed. She put the crosshairs on it, squeezed the trigger. The puff as the bullet struck the target came fast. She liked this rifle. Another flash. She centered it in the crosshairs, squeezed the trigger. A body fell. Once again, she was a machine – aim, shoot, aim, shoot. Through the NV, she watched her unit advance. She was in the zone. She loved this job.

Her radio crackled. "Time to go home," Lieutenant Harvey said.

Back in the debrief room, the lieutenant stood before his unit. "Nice job. We did well."

"What was that about?" asked Kiki. "We went in there, killed a couple of guys and left. What did we do?" Heads nodded around her.

"Okay, it was a training mission," said Harvey. "We wanted you to see what the landscape was like."

"It was ugly," said Kiki. "When you put our asses on the line, we want to accomplish something. This was like jacking off in the bathroom."

A chuckle rippled through the briefing room at Kiki's hard-guy language.

"Okay, tomorrow night we're going for their headquarters, Palomar."

"Let's take a look at the satellite pix," said Kiki.

They were detailed and clear. "Four gun positions," said Kiki. "Looks like machineguns. Two sniper positions and a fortified gate. Are we supposed to take the installation or kill people?"

"Both," said the lieutenant.

"Not a good answer," said Kiki. "What is our goal?"

"Gang leadership is there. Kill them. Bring me back a prisoner."

"Clear enough," said Kiki. "Bring up the satellite pix again."

"I'm going to be here," she said, pointing at a knoll five hundred yards distant. "This is what I can cover." Her pointer circled the area in front of the observatory. "When you're out of this zone, I can't help you. What's this stadium with the fires?" asked Kiki, pointing to a spot.

"Rose Bowl," answered the lieutenant. "It was a quarantine center. Now it's a crematorium. So far, the gangs have left it alone. Nobody wants to go there."

"Yeah, I can understand that," said Kiki.

There were only two of them in the dorm room. PFC Dawn Mechaud, a thin blond with short hair, was also her second spotter. "What did you do in the Army?" asked Kiki.

"Analyst in Afghanistan was my last assignment."

"This the first field action you've seen?" Kiki asked.

"Yes, ma'am. I never saw anything like you this evening. I'm not sure what I'm supposed to do."

"Protect my ass, first," she laughed. Dawn joined her.

"Your primary assignment is to watch for anybody trying to gain our position. Sergeant Jackson and I will be focused on targets. That means you have to scope everything around us. If anything moves, anything closer than 300 yards, sing out. If they get inside that perimeter, we're in their kill zone. Do you understand? You know how to use that M-4 they gave you?"

"I trained and went to the range."

"We'll do some more of that. When we're out, check with me before you shoot. We're a night team. Your muzzle flash will give away our position, so only in case of an emergency."

"Got it, I think," said Dawn.

"You'll do fine. Jackson and I will take care of you." Kiki gave her a reassuring smile.

Chapter Sixty-Eight

November 2
Washington, D.C.
Situation Room

"We need to review," said the president to the assembled Cabinet. "This meeting is being broadcast to the nation to explain what's happened." How many will get the message is unknown, but we have to try, thought the president. "We will not sugarcoat the news. Let's begin with early September. Ron, please start with the cyber-attack."

Ron stood. "The attack started when our power grid began to fail. We had been hacked and numerous transformers sabotaged. Computer viruses were taking down the control systems for our distribution. We suspected North Korea as the perpetrators. These were vulnerable systems because of inadequate protection and unavailability of replacement parts. As a result, we have had sectors of the country without power since September 11. Our workarounds took care of some of the problems, but the foreign replacement parts are still suspect. In a nutshell, the system is unreliable. That is the new norm." He looked up from his notes with a grim smile.

"The power outages resulted in other utility losses, particularly water distribution. In addition to the loss of potable water, it became impossible to fight fires. Large portions of our biggest cities burned when rioters torched whole neighborhoods." Ron paused, glancing up from his notes. "Law enforcement had to initiate a shoot-on-site policy with rioters. The fatalities from power loss are large and will grow substantially. A hard winter is predicted. Our economy is a disaster, with almost all industry at a standstill. We're making nothing, we're selling nothing. The landscape of the United States is completely different from two months ago." Ron stood straight, as if to shake off the bad news he'd imparted to the country.

"Thank you, Ron for that candid report. Dr. Albertson, please give us an assessment of the bio-attack."

The doctor's face was thin and gray. Lines creased it. The last two months had been hard on him. "The first indication of the pathogen outbreak occurred in early September when people began to appear at emergency rooms with terrible rashes. We quickly realized that smallpox, thought to be eradicated in the 1970s, had reared its ugly head. The distribution of cases, simultaneously appearing in numerous cities across the country, told us this was not a natural occurrence. Also, the hemorrhagic form is not common, but we had an abnormally high percentage of those cases. This indicated a genetically modified form of the virus." He stopped. His face was grim. "Again, an indication of a bio-attack. Hemorrhagic smallpox is almost always fatal. Our losses have been monumental. It has swamped our ability to cope." Dr. Albertson stared into the camera.

"We commandeered pharmaceutical lab facilities to manufacture vaccine. That program is moving ahead. The quarantine program kept the disease from spreading, but it was devastating in the cities. We lost millions of people, millions." The doctor's head dropped, moving side to side.

"Thank you Dr. Albertson," said the president. "You did a commendable job with what you had." The president paused, unable to speak for a few moments. He looked up.

"David, please give us what the CIA has to date with respect to the situation in Russia and China."

The camera focused on CIA Director David Kennedy. "Little news is coming out of China or Russia. As you know, China invaded Russia, aiming to take over the oil and gas fields while Russia was preoccupied with an invasion of Eastern Europe. China's attack has slowed, and Russian forces have been redeployed to defend western Russia. President Vladimirov was attacked and suffered a debilitating injury. He will survive though his ability to rule Russia in the long term is in question. Battles continue in southern Russia. In addition, a smallpox outbreak occurred in Moscow. It is spreading. We have no details."

"Thank you, David. General Edwards, please fill us in on the situation with North Korea."

"Yes, Sir. For reasons unknown, North Korea launched four nuclear missiles. We are not sure of the target, but two of those missiles self-destructed. The other two struck Beijing, China, and Koltsovo, Russia. We estimated the power at fifty kilotons, enough to cause widespread destruction and death. The Chinese National Conference was in session at the time. All the leadership was killed, including President Qiang Min. Koltsovo, Russia was the last stockpile of smallpox virus and the suspected source of the contagion that struck the United States. It was also the largest stockpile of vaccine. Russia launched a nuclear strike against North Korea in retaliation. We do not know if the Supreme Leader survived, but we suspect not."

"Thank you." The president looked into the camera. "It is time for us to focus on our nation. We have to heal ourselves. Our economy is in shambles, we've lost more than one-third of our population. That's the bad news. Now we must concentrate on ourselves. I am pulling our armed forces back to the United States to aid in the rebuilding. Foreign threats are minimal. Europe has offered assistance and we will consider that. We must continue under Marshall Law until local governments are able to maintain the rule of law. It is critical that we pull together for the good of the country. As John Kennedy said, 'Ask not what your country can do for you, but what you can do for your country.' Never was that more true than today."

Chapter Sixty-Nine

November 27
Los Angeles, California

"Another Thanksgiving at war. Nick, I thought that was behind me, yet here we are," said Kiki.

"This is by far the bleakest Thanksgiving I've ever had," said Nick. "At least in the Sandbox they made an attempt at a turkey dinner." He stared at the mystery meat on his tray. "This is an indication of the state of our nation. In the Sandbox, we had the resources of the country behind us. Now, this is the best we can produce." He stirred the vegetable stew with his fork.

Kiki watched him. "Nick, let's call your family when we finish." That always cheered him up. It was now her family, too.

"Mom, happy Thanksgiving," said Kiki.

"Same to both of you. Stephen and his family and Brad and his family have joined us. Wish you were here."

"Kiki and I wish we were there, too."

"How is it in Los Angeles?" asked Brad.

"Pretty bad. We're taking back the city, neighborhood-by-neighborhood. It's slow going, like back in Afghanistan, but we're winning," said Kiki.

"How much longer will you be there?" asked Miriam.

"Nobody's saying," said Nick, his voice soft.

"They're afraid to give us R & R because too many people won't come back," said Kiki. "We get a day off here and there, but there's not a lot to do, except sleep. I've been on night duty, so Nick and I only get to spend meals together except for days off."

"Did you get a Thanksgiving dinner?" asked Stephen.

"Sorta," said Nick. What did you do?

"We actually had a Thanksgiving feast, with chicken instead of turkey, but Stephen did a magnificent job," said Miriam. "We're going down to the refugee camp later to offer more food to them. Listening to some of the stories, we do have a lot to be thankful for."

"They're not giving us much time on the phones, so we're going to have to go," said Nick. "Hope we'll be coming back soon. Love you all."

"Love you back," said Miriam. "Take care of yourselves. Bye."

Nick and Kiki went back to their room. At least they got to room together since they were married, thought Kiki. Well, married in the eyes of the Army even if there were no documents.

"We have things to be thankful for, too, Nick," said Kiki. "Our family seems safe and we're together."

"You're right. It's too easy to dwell on the bad."

Their lovemaking was soft and tender, each enjoying the feel and touch of the other. They fell asleep intertwined.

Kiki's mind itched so badly it hurt. Oh God. No.

"How touching. My other self who likes the flavor of love and joy is dining on you two tonight. Katherine, you give me feasts from your enemies. Once again, your name generates fear and hatred among them. As

with your enemies in Afghanistan, they will take action."

Nick and Katherine froze. It had been a month since the Director had contacted them. "I'm so pleased I could feed you," sneered Kiki. She felt her loathing of this creature rise in a hot flash.

"Ah, there is that hatred I enjoy from you. I must tell you I am developing a taste for despair. It is an emotion quite plentiful in the world today though the bitter aftertaste takes getting used to. Must go. Be cautious. Tata."

"K, I'm worried," said Nick. "It sounds like there may be another ambush attempt on your life like the one in Afghanistan." Gently Nick touched Kiki's shoulder where the bullet wound had left a scar. "That one nearly got you."

Chapter Seventy

December 7
Los Angeles

"Dawn, what do you make of these aerials of the area around downtown?" Kiki pointed at the monitor.

PFC Dawn Mechaud looked at the big-screen of the photos taken yesterday by the drone. "This night flyover shows light in the convention center," she pointed. "This entrance has guards at the doors, and shooters in posts around it. Something important there. Vehicles entering and exiting the underground parking. It's some kind of headquarters."

"Yeah, that's what the captain thought." said Kiki. "He wants to plan an assault. From the LA convention center, they control the major highways, I-10, I-110, and I-5. Where should we set up?"

Dawn studied the pictures. "K, this is risky. There are taller buildings farther out giving a field of fire, but they are nearly 1000 yards. Lots of stuff between them and our targets, too. It's not a clear field of fire. Enemy sentries on these other buildings could take shots at us, though. Dignity Hospital looks like the best site for us. It was a quarantine site, so maybe there's no bad guys in there."

"I saw it, too. New line of thought. If you were going to set a trap for us, how would you do that?"

Again, Dawn studied the photos. "They have to expect we'll try to gain control of the roads, so they know where we're going. The obvious thing is to give you the best vantage point for coverage, then plan an assault on that position. That would be the hospital." She pointed. "If they cut us off, we'll be trapped."

Kiki nodded. The building was her first choice to give the assault her best support. From the roof, she could take out the enemy shooters at the guard posts. A helicopter exit was the obvious strategy. Bet there was something planned for that, she mused.

An idea began to form. She needed to see the captain.

"Sir, got a few minutes?" Kiki said, knocking on his door.

"Come in, Russell."

"Cap, before we go in on this assault, my team needs special training."

"What kind of special training?"

"Sir, as I'm sure you're aware, this downtown assault could turn into an ambush."

"Russell, we're going in heavy, tanks and APCs."

"Yes, sir, but in order for me to be most effective, I'll need to be up high with a clear field. That position might turn into a trap for us."

"Russell, we'll have a squad protecting that building."

"Sir, have you looked at the underground access? There're utility tunnels going from building to building and under the streets. Your squad could easily get attacked from inside the building, where your armor would be useless. We'd be next on the menu."

"Russell, this attack is in the early planning stages. You've brought up some good points. What about another site for you?"

"Sir, I'll be most effective at that point. Even if you take the headquarters, there will still be rats fleeing, some of them bent on revenge."

"Russell, we could chopper you off that roof."

"Yes, sir, but it's the obvious way. I'm sure these boys thought of that and have plans. Even with an escort, it would be hard. Losing a chopper would really spoil our day."

"Yeah, I wouldn't like that."

"If they really wanted to get us, they could mine the building, bring it down with us on top. That would be bad for your squad, too."

"How long will this training take?"

"Cap, there's an airborne group in San Bernardino. A few days with them should do it."

"Airborne!" He looked up at her. I thought it was target practice. What kind of training do you need?"

Kiki explained her plan to him.

"I like it. Yeah, I'll cut you orders. We should be ready when you get back."

Chapter Seventy-One

December 14
Los Angeles

From twenty thousand feet, the city was a dark blotch speckled by the pyres at the Staples Center and other burning sites where the infected dead were cremated. The surrounding areas were quarantined, something even the rebels respected. Through her night vision, from the open door of the small plane, Kiki watched the tangle of freeways approach.

She, Dawn and Jackson lined up at the door. They activated the infrared blinkers on their backs. With the IR sensor on, they could follow each other. The green light flashed, Kiki jumped into the darkness.

During free-fall, she guided herself toward their target roof, the highest in the area. The night was calm, so wind was not an issue. She popped her chute and began to spiral down. She had to trust Dawn and Jackson to follow. If they didn't, there was nothing she could do. She circled over the edge wall, feathered out and alit, flexing her knees, then dumping the chute. Quickly, she pulled it in.

Ten seconds later, she heard a thump. Dawn had arrived. Kiki helped her gather her chute. Another thump, Jackson had landed. So far, so good. Chutes stowed, she set up the firing positions. Kiki had the AR-10 with her extended muzzle brake. It made the rifle long, but the muzzle flash would only be visible to the target. It would also be silent.

Through the night vision scope, she mapped out her targets, starting with the closest one. Though there was a chance her flash would be seen, there would be no sonic shockwave heard by those behind.

"Kickoff in ten," Jackson reminded her, tapping his watch.

Time to go to work, she thought. Kiki moved to the side of the building opposite the headquarters target. Two blocks away, the advance team of her unit moved from doorway to doorway toward the hospital. These men would secure the ground floor to prevent surprises. She had a good view of the guards posted around the convention center and the roadblocks set up on the freeways. The complex was 600 yards, easy shots for her. In the green light of the night vision, she put the crosshairs on the nearest guard's chest. She squeezed the trigger, the rifle bucked against her shoulder. The man went down.

"Nice shooting," Jackson commented.

Kiki moved to the next target. The other guards knew something was up, the silenced rifle confused them. She moved methodically from the outer posts toward the main entrance. At the edge of the parking lot, she watched the point men of her unit advance. The Armored Personnel Carrier entered the lot. From the side of the convention center, a flash streaked toward the APC. "RPG," she yelled as the rocket exploded.

"Oh God!" screamed Dawn. "All those men."

"K, it's a trap! Look at the south end of the center," yelled Jackson.

Through the NV scope, Kiki saw a stream of men flooding into the parking lot. She began picking targets.

"They're coming in from the north, too," said Dawn. The sound of gunfire erupted below them. A helicopter circled overhead trying to give cover. Two streaks arced toward it. One sped by, the other hit the body with a clang. There was no explosion. A dud. God, what were the chances. They needed a break.

"Sergeant Russell," her com unit sounded, "Lieutenant Harvey here. We're pulling back. You were right about the tunnels. My men had to withdraw. We'll be at an extraction point two blocks east and wait for you there. Look for our beacon. Out."

"Gotta go, guys," yelled Kiki. "Now!" She buckled her precious AR-10 to her chest. At the edge of the roof, they set up the three Snake Eyes Chute System mortar tubes. It was an ultra-low altitude parachute system. They strapped on the harnesses. "Ready, guys?" Kiki asked. Jackson and Dawn nodded. Kiki yanked the trigger cord.

With a dull whump, a dark streamer shot skyward. With a whoosh, it inflated, forming an airfoil. Kiki leaped from the roof. She gasped as she dropped until the airfoil caught the air with enough lift to carry her. In the green glow of her night vision, she saw the infrared light marking the rendezvous point. Glancing behind, she saw the black outline of Dawn and Jackson's chutes. She guided the chute toward it. They'd made their escape from the trap.

Chapter Seventy-Two

December 14
Los Angles

The blackout shades were drawn, giving Nick and Kiki a dark room, but sleep eluded them. With both of them on night patrols, they lived like owls, hunting at night, sleeping during the day.

"That was close, K," whispered Nick.

"It was close for you, too. If that rocket hadn't been a dud, you'd have gone down." Kiki gave him a hug.

"I'm worried about the next time," Nick sighed. "We can't dodge these bullets forever."

"Nick, I'm worried about more than that. We are supposed to be on a six-month tour. We are retaking much of Los Angeles from the gangs and warlords. The problem is we don't have the forces to occupy our objectives afterwards. Without support, they fall back into chaos. One thing I learned in the Middle East, it's not enough to recapture territory. Once we withdrew, the local government wasn't sufficiently strong enough keep it."

"Yeah, we retook the same objectives more than once," said Nick, "and Afghanistan is tiny compared to the United States."

Kiki sighed. "We had allies there to help. Our military was never trained to fight a civil action within the United States. How much longer will we be here? Where do we to go after this? Nick, I want to go home. I want things to be like they were before." She felt as if she were looking down an endless dark tunnel.

"I don't think they will ever be as they were before," said Nick, his voice thick. "It's only now I can see how delicate the system was. We allowed it to become compartmentalized because it was easy – easy to turn law enforcement over to police, easy to turn governing over to politicians, easy to turn education over to schools. We lost our sense of community and involvement. It made us vulnerable to disaster. Nowhere was this more true than in the large cities. Now we pay."

"At least during the Civil War, rebel states banded together giving the Union an enemy with a single face." said Kiki. "We've gone back to tribalism. Each territory has a leader or warlord. We fight them piece by piece. How do we do that? How do we win?" A cold chill filled Kiki's mind. Oh no, not now, she thought.

"There is that despair flavor I have learned to savor. It is not an emotion I expected to dine on from you. Surely, you do not believe things are hopeless. Not you who creates fear and hatred in your enemies. Come on, now chin up. Haha."

"I'm past caring what you like," snapped Kiki. "How much of this despair is due to your tweaking and directing?"

"Actually, I had to do very little. The bio-attack and cyber-attack took a little push to raise the hatred level, but once that happened, all I have had to do is enjoy. The Russian invasion of Europe was a bit of my doing. Vladimirov's ego is so great, it was not hard for him to believe he could succeed. Those namby-pamby parts of me who enjoy the taste of love and happiness are going hungry in your world today. If it is any consolation to you, my feasting in Russia

and Asia is much greater than in the United States. The leaders are losing control and not without a lot of blood. Tasty for me, not so good for you humans. I find Russian leader Vladimirov's fear particularly delicious, as he has not felt it for decades. Sharks are closing in. The hatred they feel for him is especially sharp. I must go."

"I can't say I'm sorry to see you feeding on them," said Kiki, "or the Chinese leaders, for that matter."

"Alas, they succumbed to the pathogen they used to infect much of the world. They are off my menu. By the way, good escape last night. You pushed the hatred toward you up another notch. The bounty has doubled. A little greed exists within your own ranks. Be careful. Tata for now."

"Kiki, we have to get out of here," said Nick.

"Yeah, but we can't desert."

"With a bounty on your head, who can we trust? I'm calling in a marker tomorrow," said Nick.

Chapter Seventy-Three

December 21
Casa Grande, Arizona

A blast of crisp desert air struck them as the helicopter lifted off the Sabino driveway. Miriam gave a Nick a hug. "It's so good to have you home. I've been worried about you and Katherine."

"It's good to be home, Mom." Nick looked around. Winter in Casa Grande was a primo time to be here.

"Are you on Christmas leave?" asked Stephen.

"Longer than that," said Nick. "We've been released from active duty. We're home now."

"Nick, you always come in with a splash. Was that Ron Carson on the helicopter with you?" asked Stephen.

"Yeah. He arranged our return."

"Well, just in time." Stephen slapped Nick on the back. "The Christmas party starts in an hour. Everybody will be glad to see you."

Nick and Kiki circulated among the guests as Christmas music played in the background. The punch bowl had been refilled with eggnog twice, and the guests were showing the effects. It was kickass good and strong.

"Nick, Kiki, good to see you," said Brad.

"Good to be back," said Nick, giving him a hug. Kiki was smothered in his embrace.

"I saw the chopper land and thought it might be you. Home on leave?"

"No, Brad. We've been released from duty." A puzzled look crossed Brad's face. "Kiki was becoming too effective. The rebels put a bounty on her," Nick pulled her to his side. "We weren't sure the Army could protect her."

Brad's face clouded. "We've had problems here, too. Not all of our volunteers are out for the community good. We caught five stealing, and a few gang members recruiting."

"What did you do with them?" asked Nick.

"The thieves are in a forced labor pool. The gangbangers are dead. We no longer have the luxury of housing and feeding idle prisoners."

"The new harsh reality," said Kiki. Nick and Brad nodded.

"These gangs have long arms. Think they'll come after you here?" asked Brad.

"If they do," said Kiki, "it'll tell us something about their data mining capabilities. I am always listed as Katherine Russell, home address a PO box in Marana, no ties to Casa Grande."

"But are there records of us?" asked Nick.

"Nothing official, but our relationship was common knowledge," said Kiki. "Yeah, they could find me. I'm not running."

"We're a community, Kiki," said Brad. "We watch out for each other."

Kiki lay next to Nick, staring at the darkened ceiling. Their lovemaking had been slow and sensuous. "It was a nice party." She snuggled up to Nick, her fingers tracing a path across his chest. "This town is so different from LA. It's nice to be here."

Nick felt her stiffen.

"Nick, I love you, and living in Casa Grande could be wonderful, though I'm not sure what I would be doing." Kiki let out a sigh. "This life isn't me. It would be a repeat of my life on the ranch with Chet. I couldn't do that then. I can't do that now. In my heart, I'm a soldier."

"K, you could adapt. You could...."

"Nick when I'm behind that rifle, I'm alive. When I'm here, I'm waiting for the next assignment. The hardest part is you. You have a family here. You have a life here that you love, helping people, becoming a doctor. I'm not like your mother, willing to spend my life supporting you."

But how can I leave you? Kiki wondered. The pain of leaving Chet and Lindy and her parents stung. Her eyes watered.

"Nick, I'm not going to wait for them to come after me. I'm not going to put others in danger because of me. My family was killed because of me."

"K, do not put this on yourself. It was evil men who killed your family. It's evil men who are after you now." Nick reached for her.

Kiki pulled away. "I have only two choices, Nick. I can return to my ranch and wait for them to find me, or I can go after them. If I wait for them, there will be a string of people trying to collect. It won't end. Since I'm going to be sought wherever I am, I will become the hunter and on their grounds. It's the only way to stop this." Kiki turned toward him, her hand seeking his.

"I guess I knew this was coming, but hoped..." Nick stopped, swallowed. "I expected nothing less. I could never let you go. We go after them, K. We're together, remember. We're a team." Nick pulled her to him. This time she came willingly, nestling into his arms. "We should talk to Ron."

Chapter Seventy-Four

January 18
Oval Office.
Washington, DC

President Donaldson turned his gaze from the White House lawn to Ron Carson. "Ron, I've grown close to you during this crisis. I trust your judgment. I like your analytical mind. So, I want to bounce some things back-and-forth, just you and me, before we meet with the Cabinet and of course the State of the Union address."

The president looked exhausted. He had aged markedly, lines deeply etched in his face, his hair nearly all gray.

"Thank you, Mr. President. We came through trying times."

"I have two big questions to discuss. First, what did we learn, and second where are we going? I wanted your opinion and ideas before we start a public debate."

Ron took a deep breath. "Mr. President, one thing we've learned is how unprepared we were for unconventional devastating attacks. Numerous people raised alarms, but our money for defense went into high-tech systems for conventional war. They were not effective in a bio-attack, and they were not effective in the cyber-war because the military was not the target."

"You're right, Ron, but it's always easier to Monday morning quarterback. We ignored warnings and threats."

"Mr. President," began Ron, "I've been thinking about this for a long time. A more basic lesson has become clear. This battle was an extension of a terrorist campaign using people as tools to disrupt and destabilize the government. The killing is merely the tool to create loss of faith. In this case, not only was that loss of trust achieved, but the economy was a direct target."

The president nodded. "It wasn't the territory of the United States that was attacked. Our position in the world has been destroyed. We will not be an economic power for years, perhaps decades."

"Sir, Ronald Reagan waged economic war against the old USSR, driving them to spend themselves into ruin. He built up our weapon systems, forcing the USSR to match us. Their economy couldn't sustain that. We won without firing a shot or invading. But we got a huge military-industrial complex that is our economic ogre. To justify its existence, we have tried to police and control the rest of the world. It certainly hasn't brought stability or peace."

"That's rather critical, don't you think?"

"Perhaps so," agreed Ron.

"What else did we learn?"

"It's apparent our large cities were precariously balanced on the logistics of supply – utilities, food, health services. A break in that logistical train caused the thin veneer of civilization to be stripped away. The high population concentration of the cities made them vulnerable to bio-attack. We told people to stay in their houses to prevent the spread of disease and then told them to go to distribution centers for food and water. We've lost credibility. Many people just decided to give up."

"On the flip side," said the president, "the smaller cities and towns pulled together. The specialization roles we fell into like law enforcement, city services and government management led to the *we/they* mentality. The smaller communities quickly learned the *we* was the community, and the *they* were outsiders. There is a new sense of community and participation."

"Yes, sir, but they built barricades to keep out the savages. Refugees are turned away to keep from swamping their resources. It's a cold new world. In some ways it's a lot like the very early days of this country, when the small towns were the bastions of growth in a sea of wilderness."

The president was silent as he shared Ron's vision of mansions such as Mt. Vernon and Monticello representing self-supporting islands of civilization.

"Mr. President, it's clear that decentralization is where we are headed whether we want to or not. The lesson is that centralization leads to vulnerability."

"So where do you see us heading, Ron?"

"Mr. President, the country is under Marshall Law. Idaho, Montana, and Wyoming are members of the United States only in name. Federal law enforcement officers are needed in other areas. If we try to exert federal law in those states, they will withdraw from the Union."

Tears appeared in the president's eyes. The Union could fall apart.

"Mr. President, California is in open rebellion. If the gangs unite under a strong leader, it will be lost. We don't have the manpower to occupy both the west coast and the east coast."

God! thought the president. They may be forced to triage the country. He looked at Ron. "Democracy will not be restored until an effective government is in place, but the Union must prevail."

"Yes, sir. The democracy that emerges will not be what we had before," said Carson.

The president looked thoughtful. "In some ways, we are on the frontier. We need a strong dictatorship to rebuild, but with a loose central control. The small cities are becoming more independent. For now, they need to. Eventually we will go back to a democratic government. I think the 10th Ammendment to the Constitution limiting the reach of the federal government will play a much stronger role."

"We have tools that will help," said Ron. "The internet and social media will allow us to unite while dispersed. We will no longer need huge office buildings, large cities and commercial centers."

"Yeah, the Arab Spring and the Turkish coup attempt were lessons in using and controlling social media," affirmed the president.

"The Plain states, the Midwest, the Central states and much of the south weathered this disaster well," noted Ron. "We must focus and stabilize there first. We must revive productivity. With so many of our people lost, mechanization and robotics will help."

"Where's the fly in the ointment?" asked the president.

"The world has changed drastically," noted Ron. "We must adapt to new values."

"Ron, we have to regain control of our coasts. Much of the east coast is still without power. Winter and starvation have taken a terrible toll."

"Yes sir. In hindsight, our efforts to bring back power to the cities was misspent. We have to get back to being a producing country. We have to grow, mine and manufacture."

"We need our coasts back. We can't import or export without those ports. What about the west coast?"

"True," said Ron. "But the world stage has changed. China and Russia lost their armies and their leadership. It will be at least a decade before they represent viable economies. We want the Pacific ports back, but they are not as critical as the Atlantic and Gulf ports for now. Europe is where our markets lie. We do not have the resources to take back the whole country today."

A troubled look came over the president's face. "Whatever groups hold the territories, they must uphold the Constitution. We need to see to that. My greatest fear is that religious groups will take over and force their beliefs and intolerance on the population. It's what we've seen repeatedly in the Mideast and throughout history. More people have been killed in the name of God than any other cause."

"Except for this last war, sir."

"Perhaps it is time to push harder for a world government, so events like the ones we've been through won't happen again. The United Nations will be very different."

"The problem, sir, is what form of government that would be. People don't know what's best for their nation, only for themselves."

"Yes, people always seem to get in the way," sighed the president. "It will be awhile before we hold an election. In the meantime, we'll operate under a benevolent dictatorship. Help keep me benevolent, Ron."

Epilogue

January 31
Casa Grande

Secretary of Interior Ron Carson sat on the Sabino patio with Kiki and Nick. The sky was clear of clouds and the deep blue of a winter desert day.

"Thanks for coming," said Kiki. "We needed to talk away from any other ears. It's important."

"I appreciate the invitation. The weather is certainly nicer here than in Washington D.C. How's retirement going?"

"That's what we wanted to talk to you about," said Nick.

"Thanks for getting us out of LA. You probably saved my life, Mr. Secretary," said Kiki.

"We're past that Mr. Secretary stuff. Ron will do."

"Ron, the bounty on my head makes everywhere unsafe for me, and staying here endangers those I love. I can't do that, nor can I hide." Kiki looked at Nick. "We want to go back and fight these bastards."

Nick nodded.

"We don't have any forces fighting there," said Ron. "Our military installations like Camp Pendleton, San Diego Naval Station and Travis Air Force Base are isolated. They are the only pockets of the United States remaining in California."

"We understand that," said Nick. "We listened to the president's State of the Union speech. We understand the efforts of the government are not focused on California." He looked at Kiki, taking her hand. "We hope that giving up California is temporary. We would go in as a guerilla team to harass the gangs."

"Ron, I'm going to be in danger. At least there I'll know where it's coming from. We can strike back."

Ron looked thoughtful. "Let me get General Edwards on the line." Within minutes, the general was on speakerphone.

"Nick, Katherine, it's good to talk to you. Again, I want to thank you for your service. We would be in much worse shape today if we hadn't had it."

"You're welcome, sir," said Kiki. "General, Nick and I want to go back into LA as a guerilla team. We'll let Ron fill you in later on the background, but we feel we can be effective in harassing the gangs."

"I'm sure you can. We have no operations going at present. The president has a tacit agreement stating we won't fight against the gangs if they leave our military installations alone. Once those gangs organize under a single ruling body, he will sign a treaty. California will become a country." The general's voice was low, almost a growl. "We just don't have the forces to cover the country. Once we have the east coast back, we'll retake California."

"Perhaps we could slow down the efforts to organize the gangs," said Kiki.

"I'm sure you could," said Ron. "Hopefully until the government is strong enough to retake California," he added in a soft voice.

"Hmmm. Let me think about this out loud. These are only ideas to kick around, so don't hold me to anything. This idea has been considered since it looked like we were going to cede California, but I can't talk about that. We would not be able to give you any open support, but we could give you supplies and intel from Pendleton. We could fly you out of Pendleton and drop you on the beach near Pt. Mugu. Our satellites show a lot of burned-out areas with nobody stirring."

"General, it's imperative that this is kept quiet. With the price on Kiki's head, we don't know who can be trusted."

At least with just the two of them, the danger of betrayal was limited, thought Kiki. A team of two seemed awfully small when arrayed against an army. But then, they weren't fighting an army. She had a specific target.

"You're right," observed the general. "We probably shouldn't inform the president, either, should we, Ron?"

"No, general. It's best if he can deny any knowledge."

"Nick, Katherine, your asses are really going to be hanging out on this," said the general.

They nodded. "We know, sir, but that's how it has to be," said Kiki.

For a preview of the next "Dead" book, turn the page. This book is in the early stages. The title and text may change, but the theme will prevail. Nick and Kiki ride again!

R. L. Clayton

Dead Again
R. L. Clayton

Prologue

Katherine "Kiki" Russell placed her crosshairs on the bearded figure standing at the dais. His black leather vest was adorned with chains and silver studs, his chest heavily tattooed. In his case, his scraggly beard was an improvement as it covered up more of the scars on his ugly face. He was a secondary target. Sean Gallen hadn't appeared yet.

The silenced .22 would give her time for three or four shots before anybody on the stage understood what was happening, but the low power cartridge meant all the shots had to be headshots. Her plan was extremely dangerous. She was inside the arena, high up in the rafters, and her escape was through a hatch to the roof. Her blind was a gutted air conditioning system, complete with a battery operated motor to keep it humming and vibrating during any search for the assassin, something sure to follow this assault.

Kiki's partner, Nick Sabino, would fire shots through a glass door as a diversion. He had no targets on the stage. He was four-hundred yards away from her position with a clear escape route. When things settled down after the manhunt, she would use the Snake Eyes Low Level paraglider system to fly from the top of the six-story dome to their egress point. Four days ago, she and Nick, disguised as facilities repairmen, had moved their equipment in. Nick left, she stayed hidden within the A/C unit. She had stashed her SELL paraglider on the roof night before last.

On the stage were the warlords of the new country, Kalifornia Republik. Sean Gallen was trying to unite them with himself as leader. If he succeeded, it was possible Idaho, Wyoming and Montana would seek to join. A cheer erupted from the crowd.

No Sean. She could wait no longer. Though she was well hidden, Nick could be found by a roving patrol. Kiki squeezed off her first shot as Nick's shot smashed the glass. The speaker's right eye disappeared. He slumped. One of the other warlords seated behind him jumped up to assist. Kiki ignored him. With the clamor of rising panic, she could get in more shots. Screams filled the arena. People scrambled for cover. Kiki sighted on a figure huddled behind a chair on the stage. He collapsed. Another of Nick's shots crashed through the glass door.

Below, figures raced up the stairs, guns waving. Brave but foolish, she thought. Kiki ignored them. One man jumped up, yelling for the guards to "Get that cabrón son of a bitch."

Nick fired again. Kiki put a bullet through the screaming man's temple.

"They're streaming out into the parking lot," Nick's voice came over her com unit. "I got enough time for one more shot."

"Take it. This will be my last one, too," Kiki murmured. Damn! Sean Gallen was tall and thin with blond hair. He hadn't been on stage. Was he even here?

A giant of a man with an art gallery of tattoos on his bare torso was directing others in the chaos. She put a shot through his ear as Nick's last shot rang out.

Kiki closed the firing-slot. Nothing to do but wait now – maybe more than a day. In the total darkness, she relaxed in the fetal position – all the room allowed in the a/c box. She sipped water sparingly. Too much water and she'd be testing her astronaut diapers.

During the chaos of the Bio-Cyber war, outlaw motorcycle gangs, drug gangs and ethnic gangs had taken over, waging open warfare against law enforcement, the military and each other. As the United States didn't have the resources to fight the insurgents in two wars a continent apart, the decision was made to focus on the eastern United States, and let the gangs and warlords take over California, temporarily. Kiki was part of the original U. S. Army effort to retake California, but got pulled back. She was out of the war and safe in Casa Grande, Arizona. Then she found out Sean Gallen, leader of the Charon's Children outlaw motorcycle gang had put a price on her head, a price high enough that they would find her. Her presence would endanger those she loved. It had happened before. Her family had been brutally murdered because of her. Not this time. She and Nick were going after the man who wanted her dead.

"I'm away," came Nick's whisper through her com. "I'll let you know when things have calmed down. Sleep tight."

Yeah, Kiki thought. As if. Footfalls vibrated the catwalk beside her box. She tensed, holding the silenced pistol to her chest. If her hidey-hole was discovered, she'd have to shoot her way out. Chances of that succeeding were remote.

She heard the searcher move away. The darkness within her metal cocoon was timeless.